Praise for THE O

A vivid accounting of a too frequent tragedy of ̶ ̶ ̶ ̶ ̶ ̶ ̶ ̶ ̶ ̶ ̶ .̶.̶.̶o̶n̶ era. Chet overcame abuse, neglect and loneliness to become a successful adult and a solid American family man. He was lucky; many were not.

> Cecil D. Andrus
> Former Governor of Idaho
> and U.S. Secretary of the Interior

A poignant tale of one man's search for happiness in the building of a family of his own. A "must read" for every Idahoan.

> Tom Sweeney
> Author of "Out of the Gate"
> Dutch Oven Cafe 'Idaho Philosopher'

Courage comes with many faces and many forms. Writing 'The Orphan' and exposing his soul reveals a Chet Hosac who exemplifies courage. Engrossing, poignant, a delightful story of a cast away child who becomes a man.

> Kermit W. (Andy) Andrus
> Colonel, USMC (Retired)

My good friend Chet Hosac has done what we all should do—share our life stories with the world. He has enriched all of us by the example of his tenacity, humanity, and capacity for loving. The sweep of his life story stimulates thoughts about this century in American history and society. It is down to earth, but an upbeat story we need more of.

> Byron Johnson
> Idaho Supreme Court Justice

This book is a collection of life and hazards and love and the way it was in the days before and after the depression and when World War II changed everyone's life forever. It brings out the details of farming and mining to those who have not had the opportunity to experience it. I found it very refreshing and interesting.

> A. Dale McMurtrey
> Past Potentate of the El Korah Shrine
> Former owner, Summers Funeral Home

THE

ORPHAN

Throughout the world, children become ORPHANS due to circumstances beyond
their control: wars, fatal accidents or even abandonment.
This is the story of one such orphan and his journey
through almost eighty years of life.

A NOVEL

BY

CHET HOSAC

© 1999 by Chet Hosac

THE ORPHAN: A Novel by Chet Hosac

This book is a work of fiction, based in part on actual events.

Library of Congress Number: 98-075296

Fiction

International Standard Book Number (ISBN): 1-887747-23-0

Printed in the United States

Second Printing 2001

This book is published by:

Chet Hosac
5820 N. Cloud Nine Drive
Boise, Idaho 83714
(208) 378–7088

DEDICATION

This book is dedicated to all the children brought into the world
and then discarded, for whatever reason.

Especially those who had the innate courage to survive.

Oct 27, 2001

Thanks

[signature]

ACKNOWLEDGMENTS

To Lorraine, for all the Love, Support and Encouragement given me throughout our lifetime together; plus knowing how to punctuate and spell.

To Lorry Roberts, Legendary Publishing, for her guidance.

And to my daughter Kay Carter and to her daughter Kimberly Carter-Cram, for all their help and encouragement.

THE ORPHAN

INTRODUCTION

The period referred to in this book was during the great depression of the 1930's. Unless one had lived through this terrible time it would be impossible to understand the desperation felt by men trying to care for their families against odds that were insurmountable. There were no jobs and in the great cities the only food to be found came from long bread lines. Men, by the hundreds, rode the freight trains. Called Hobos and Bums, they were considered outcasts by society. Most were fine, decent men and were suffering shame and abuse simply because they had heard a rumor of a job some place down the road. A classic depression statement was "Write, when you find work."

The breakdown of the stable family structure was felt by thousands of children who found themselves roaming the streets, stealing, living in abandoned houses and subjected to all forms of abuse just to survive. Compassionate people all across America became aware of this situation and sacrificed time and money, hoping to save the children.

It started with single individuals like Mrs. Shields who had a small home on Allumbaugh Lane in Boise, Idaho and went all the way to the Children's Home Finding and Aid Society of Idaho created and built by the efforts of many civic minded citizens. Among them were the Governor of the State, Frank R. Gooding and Mrs. Cynthia A. Mann, who generously donated the land on Warm Springs Avenue, where the Children's Home was to be built. The State of Idaho appropriated $20,000.00 which was matched by the caring people of the State. Table Rock Quarry located east of the city of Boise provided the stone and the Home was built in the 1930's. Hundreds of children were taken in, given shelter and in many cases placed in foster homes, becoming a loved member of a family.

As a child, I was shuttled from one family to another, finally ending up along with several other children in a foster home. The foster home was on Allumbaugh Lane in Boise, Idaho and was run by Mrs. Shields. She was a fine Christian lady who did her best to feed and clothe us.

Mrs. Shield's House

Cole School

I was in the fourth grade at Cole School, located at the corner of Cole Road and what is now Fairview Avenue. At that time the school was surrounded by pasture. Mrs. Shields tried to take in younger children because she wanted to share as much food and care as she was financially and physically able to do.

My parents couldn't or wouldn't pay the small amount necessary for my keep at Mrs. Shields. As a result, I was then considered an abandoned child, and placed in the Children's Home by the State authorities. My parents signed legal papers making me eligible for adoption. It is a tragedy for a child to lose his parents; but it is a much greater tragedy when a child becomes an ORPHAN, through the legal process initiated by his own biological Father and Mother.

THE CHILDREN'S HOME FINDING AND AID SOCIETY OF IDAHO

INCORPORATED MAY, 1908

RECEIVING HOMES
704 Warm Springs Avenue, Boise
1806 Eighteenth Avenue, Lewiston

Fairfield, Idaho Oct. 23rd- 1931

The undersigned being solicitous that their child Chester Hosac born at Gooding, Idaho on Aug. 12th-1919 , and who is now 12 years of age, should receive the benefits and advantages of THE CHILDREN'S HOME FINDING AND AID SOCIETY OF IDAHO, and said Society, through its authorized agents, being willing to receive and provide for a Christian home, with all its advantages of education, and to be fitted for the requirements of life:

We the undersigned, the parents of said child do hereby surrender him to said Society and promise not to interfere in the his management in any respect whatever, nor to visit him without the consent of the State Superintendent of the Society. And in consideration of the benefits guaranteed by the said Society in thus providing for child, do relinquish all right and claim to the child herein named and his services until he arrive at full age. And we agree not to ask or receive any consideration for the services of said child, or seek to effect his removal from the home in which he may be placed by the agents of said Society. We also hereby state that the child named above was born in wedlock, and that his name is William Chester Hosac whose residence (if alive) is Boise, Idaho

Witness our hands and seal at Fairfield, Idaho this 23rd day of October 1931.

Harry Hosac
Hester Hosac

Witness

State of Idaho
Camas County } ss.

I hereby certify that this day appeared before me, the undersigned a Notary Public in and for said County and State Harry Hosac and Hester Hosac (husband and wife) who are me personally known to be the identical persons whose name is signed to the foregoing instrument as parents to the child therein named, and that they acknowledged the instrument to be their voluntary act and deed for the uses and purposes therein named.

IN TESTIMONY WHEREOF, Witness my hand and seal at Fairfield Idaho in said County, this 23rd day of October A.D 1931.

Notary Public for Camas County, Idaho State.

Typically this child is emotionally scarred, feeling abandoned, neglected and unloved.

Fortunate indeed is a child of this background, who, for reasons unknown grows into a stable and acceptable life.

CONTENTS

CHAPTER 1
LIFE IN A CHILDREN'S HOME

LONELINESS

Sometimes now I find
myself just sitting,
thinking of the past and
wondering where the years have gone.
I dwell on my childhood
though it was never true.
I had no real childhood
Such as you.

Loneliness as a child
makes loneliness in a man,
never to be overcome,
a secret place of sorrow.
Loneliness with cold and hunger
leaves no joy for tomorrow.

But the years do pass
and tomorrows come,
bringing a measure of hope
for the needed acceptance
by someone, anyone,
you think may care,
whether you are still alive
and hopes you will survive
while wondering where.

Finally I've come around
to this time in life.
I'm certainly not alone,
and the wonder is still there.
How did it all happen?
Was it the faith of a girl
finally allowing me a share
of some of the good things?
I really don't care!

The Children's Home was an impressive building and had been designed by the State's leading architectural firm, Tourtellote & Hummel. It was staffed with caring and compassionate ladies who insisted on proper behavior. Lillian Carse and Kathryn Wolf, Superintendent, were active in lobbying for good adoptive laws that matched orphan children to acceptable parents. I seem to remember a Mrs. Young, whose son had made her a fancy inlaid paddle, in his woodworking class at school. I'm not sure about her name, but I am positive about the paddle's efficiency.

Some of the children were true orphans having lost both parents due to accidents or other causes. Some were from broken homes; but a great many came from families who simply could not find employment to buy food and provide care for them.

In my case my parents had just given me away.

I can't say that I am too unhappy in the home; yet even the thought of someone wanting me for their very own child would create a surge of joy in my heart. There were several boys like me in the home and occasionally a

The Children's Home

man and his wife would come to adopt one of us. When this happened six or eight of us were lined up along the wall and the couple would look us over and then select the one they liked. We were always severely cautioned not to speak unless asked a question. But Oh! How we would plead with our eyes, "Take me, take me!", trying so hard to project our whole being into a permanent place in their hearts. How terrible the disappointment would be when another boy was chosen. Especially when the woman had tears in her eyes as she looked at the rest of us standing there; and you knew there was enough love in her heart for all of us.

My first experience at being selected was when a kindly looking man and his wife picked me. They had a truck garden farm close to a small town in eastern Idaho. What superiority I now felt over the other boys! I had been chosen and they had not, yet my joy was mixed with a haunting sadness. These boys were my family, and although it could never be the same as a real family, still we had an association of mutual loneliness and need which bonded us together. Now I was breaking that bond and the other boys stood apart from me, drawing on their group for strength, with each of them wishing it were he who had been chosen. I stood alone, filled one moment with wild exaltation, and the next with a feeling of loss.

I spent many hours in my new family's vegetable gardens, hoeing weeds and thinning plants. They had raised eight children and I soon realized that they had used up all the love they had for children. This became obvious when, at the end of the long hot summer, and the conclusion of the vegetable harvest, I was brought back to Boise and deposited on the steps of the Children's Home.

After my own parents' rejection, and this second rejection, the first feelings of guilt entered my mind. I began to think that it was my fault that I could not be loved. There are many forms of abuse of a child and not all are sexual. It can be a rejection so severe that the child experiences something comparable to that of a rape, especially if the rejection is done by a loved family member. Self esteem can be destroyed; with a child feeling he did something wrong and is being punished. So when a second couple, Mr. and Mrs. Jackson, took me out of the Home, I was determined to do better.

The Jacksons lived on a farm close to the small town of Melba, Idaho in a two story house that had no central heating or plumbing. Both bedrooms were upstairs and my room was across the hall from Mr. and Mrs. Jackson's room. Mr. Jackson was very firm in telling me that I was expected to get up when called. I found out he meant just that, when on the first morning after I went back to sleep, I was yanked out of bed. I was so scared that I never let that happen again. I awoke some mornings and found that the top of my quilt was covered with frost. I hated to get up.

I was to help milk the cows, feed the hogs and help with all other chores that needed to be done. The farm had eighty acres planted in alfalfa hay for the milk cows and grain for the hogs. The Jacksons both worked very hard. Each of them wore a pair of bib overalls with suspenders and an old felt hat with a wide sloppy brim. When Mrs. Jackson was helping milk or working outside it was difficult to tell them apart.

The kitchen was on the main floor of the house and was dominated by a huge wood burning cook stove. A wood box sat at one end of the stove and one of my chores was to keep this box filled with pine wood that had been sawed and split, ready to be used, and enough kindling to start the fire. If anything made getting up worthwhile, it was the anticipation of getting the fire going to get warm.

I had learned to love that stove. I would quickly shake its grates to sift the ashes down in the pan, crumple up yesterday's newspaper, place the kindling with two or three sticks of wood on top, open the damper, then light the paper.

There was no inside bathroom in the house. In rural areas, indoor plumbing was a luxury and most farm houses used a small structure set over a hole dug in the ground for their bathroom. It was called an outhouse. Inside the outhouse, was a bench usually with two circular holes cut approximately twelve inches in diameter. It was freezing cold to your bare bottom in the winter and hot and smelly in the summer. Toilet paper was provided from the pages of a Montgomery Ward Catalog. With the fragrance and flies that also occupied the outhouse, as little time as possible was spent inside.

The water supply for the house came from another large hole, preferable dug uphill from the outhouse, so that no seepage from the outhouse would contaminate the house water. This was called a cistern and the sides and bottom were plastered to hold water. During the summer, irrigation water was run through a trench, approximately twelve inches deep and twelve inches wide, which was filled with sand, and helped to purify the water.

This method was also quite effective in straining garden snakes and frogs from the irrigation water before it entered the cistern. In the winter months, it was necessary to hook up a team of horses to a hay wagon and carrying a large tank, go to the nearest town for water to be put in the cistern. The water used in the house was pumped from the cistern to the kitchen sink with a pitcher pump. This pump had a twelve inch handle and when raised up and down, could suck water from the cistern.

We drank this water along with drinking raw milk, that had been strained from the milk bucket into containers set in the ice box. The cream would rise to the top and was used to make the best ice cream ever eaten. No one got sick from these practices and evidently we built up a resistance to whatever bugs the water or milk contained. Years later though I drank some raw milk for old times sake, and it made me sick.

Going to the outhouse was a ritual for all of us, and sometimes I had to get up and go during the night. How I hated it when I had to! I would lay there in my warm bed as long as possible, thinking about how cold and dark it was outside, and wishing there were some other way. But there wasn't, so finally I would jump up, slip on my pants and shoes, run downstairs, grab the flashlight and get it over with. Once I stopped just outside the door to relieve myself, but there was snow on the ground, and the next morning it was plain to everyone what I had done. Mr. Jackson didn't say anything, but I was ashamed and never did it again

In the mornings I knew that by the time I made my dash outside and back, the stove would begin to talk to me. We had become friends, this stove and I, and this was my very own time. This was the time before Mr. and Mrs. Jackson got up, when the stove crackled and popped and began to share its warmth, just for me alone. How delicious it was to feel its heat begin to spread; and, as I opened its lids to put in more wood, its fiery soul scorched my face, while its voice roared up the chimney with throaty laughter. I would pull up a hard straight- backed kitchen chair, open the oven door, place my feet in its mouth, and sit there together, this stove and I, with a few moments to dream, while I soaked up its lovely warmth to the very marrow of my bones. I dreamt of a real home. In my drowsiness I would see a real mother and father. Sometimes I would see a whole family, parents, brothers and sisters all sitting around a table; and I was there too. I never felt sure that I belonged, but I waited; and, when no one told me to leave and everyone seemed to love and want me, I began to think that I really belonged and maybe I would get to stay.

By now Mr. and Mrs. Jackson were getting up; and this was the end of my time. Now, I would have to put on my shoes and socks, warm my coat for a moment in front of my friend, and go out to bring in the cows. We all three milked, so by the time I got out to the pasture and drove the cows to the barn, Mr. and Mrs. Jackson were dressed and waiting at the barn.

How very still it would be outside! There wasn't a sound any place around. The sky was filled with a million pinpoints of light that seemed to wink on and off as you watched. There were patches of snow on the ground and when you walked over one of these patches your shoes made a crisp, squeaky sound. It must be very cold.

Some of the cows would hear me coming, and get up before I could see them in the dark. They always relieved themselves as soon as they stood up and the morning stillness was broken by the plopping sound this made. Then they would start toward the barn, having long since learned and resigned themselves to this purpose in life. But there were always a few who must have felt like I did earlier. They didn't really try to hide; but I think they hated to be found and have to get up. As I swung the flashlight around and finally saw their eyes reflected in its beam, I would feel a little sorry that I had to go over and sometimes kick them on the rump to get them on their feet. Then they would stand with a grunt and sigh and relieve themselves as they started toward the barn.

The barn was built with a high center-peaked roof and flat sloping sides. One whole side was made up of stalls where the horses were kept. On the wall behind the horses were pegs on which to hang the harnesses. The horses were kept in the barn all the time during the winter months; and one of my jobs was to pitch out their manure through a small, square window, cut just for this purpose into the side of the barn. By spring these manure piles were higher than the window itself and had to be moved back away from the window. Then these same horses would pull a manure spreader and haul their manure away to spread on the fields.

The center of the barn was filled with loose hay and I knew that while I was getting the cows, Mr. Jackson had already pitched the mangers full of hay for the cows to eat while we milked. It was a good bribe and the cows all crowded around the door waiting to get in. This side of the barn had twenty stanchions in a row. They were made by placing a single 2 x 4 between two parallel 2 x 4's on the bottom, next to another 2 x 4 fastened solid between the bottom 2 x 4's and also the top parallel 2 x 4's. The single 2 x 4 would pivot effectively locking the cow into place. When the cows were milked a pin was pulled freeing their heads, and they would leave the barn.

When Mr. Jackson opened the door, the cows would each crowd into a stanchion for the hay, and be locked into place. Most of the cows didn't care where they stood, but some of them had their very own place, and if another cow got in their stanchion they would lower their head and butt the other cow in the side to knock her out of the way. This always caused a lot of confusion. It was always done by one of the cows that I had to look for. I wondered if they had thought about it, and were using this way to show their resentment. Finally they were all locked into place and we started to milk. The barn was finally getting warm from the animal heat. I had to learn to milk when I first came here. I sat on a stool and tried to coax milk from the teats of an old and patient Holstein cow. Her udder was huge and almost touched the ground and her teats were as big as my wrists. It seemed impossible but gradually I learned to squeeze with a rippling pressure starting with the middle of my thumb and first finger and then following with the other fingers, forcing the milk out the end. I learned other lessons too. I learned to hold her tail against her leg with my knee because she seemed to delight in standing quietly, then suddenly flicking her manure coated tail across my face. I learned the hard way to keep my fingernails trimmed. Some things she would not tolerate, even with all her patience, such as being pinched by long fingernails. She let me know this one day by kicking me clear against the wall behind her, leaving me drenched with the amount of milk that I had managed to squeeze out of her. But I did learn and I never forgot again.

I didn't mind milking. I could lay my head against the cows warm flank and relax, while at the same time keeping up a steady rhythmic cadence with the streams of milk flowing into a bucket held between my knees. The sound of the milk hitting the pail and its fresh warm smell, mingled with the odors and sounds of the cows chewing their hay, created a hypnotic setting that was perfect for day dreaming.

Cats were a very necessary part of this operation and there were three or four in the barn. These were not pets but working cats which controlled the continuous hordes of mice that came in from the fields and multiplied. The cats also multiplied and sometimes a litter had to be drowned. The cats were wild and had never been petted, but they would come up close enough, if Mr. Jackson wasn't looking, for me to squirt milk into their mouths. I had become quite accurate and they licked their lips with great pleasure.

By now I was a good fast milker and could finish my fifteen cows almost as fast as Mr. Jackson did his. Mrs. Jackson milked ten of the cows, then went to the house to start breakfast. There were 40 cows altogether and it would take us two hours to gather them, milk them and turn them back out to pasture. As the buckets were filled the milk was strained into ten gallon milk cans, ready for the milk truck, which will be here soon so we have to finish quickly. These trucks and milk routes were privately owned and could be bought or sold like any other business. Some of them were owned by the drivers themselves. They were strong men who could set a ten gallon can of milk on the upper rack of their truck, with a fluid swinging motion that looked easy, but wasn't. The sound they made setting off the empty cans carried a long way on a clear cold winter morning such as this so we knew our truck was not far off.

When we finished the milking, I turned the cows out, while Mr. Jackson harnessed the team. It was just starting to get daylight now as he hitched the team to the iron-wheeled hay wagon that had been loaded with hay the day before. This hay was thrown off, with a pitchfork, across the pasture for the milk cows to eat during the day and another load was gotten ready for the next morning.

A hole had to be chopped in the ice that had frozen over the pond so the cows could drink; then the hogs had to be fed. The milk truck had left us two cans of skim milk and this was mixed with ground grain. I would mix this in old fifty five gallon barrels next to the hog pen; and now the morning quiet was gone. The air was filled with the sounds of the squealing of pigs, the bawling of cows following the hay wagon, and the noise the milk truck made as it took our milk, along with many others, to the creamery.

All of this had to be done before breakfast and the early morning cold, along with the activity would create a huge appetite. I felt like I might starve if I didn't eat soon, but before we ate I had to clean up, change clothes and get ready for school. My friend, the stove, had had its damper closed and was settled down murmuring with its work, much too busy to visit. Mr. Jackson had come into the house while I was getting ready for school, so we were finally ready to eat. The kitchen was a nice place filled with the wonderful smells of our breakfast and when we sat down to the table, covered with a red and white checkered cloth, it felt warm and cozy.

Our breakfast was almost always the same. The pork came from the very pigs I had fed. When it was time to butcher one, a very hot fire was built under a half side of a fifty five gallon barrel and filled with water. The pig was then shot between the eyes with a 22 caliber rifle. The intestines and head were removed and the pig was placed in the boiling water, which would loosen the bristles on it's skin, so that they could be scraped off. Then the pig was quartered. Some of the meat was ground, mixed with spices, then stuffed into one of the intestines, that had been thoroughly cleaned. This became sausage.

Mrs. Jackson had to parboil the salt pork to get the salt out, because it had been cured in brine. Then she would fry the pork and make gravy in the same pan. My dear, dear friend, the stove, produced a huge pan filled with beautiful hot biscuits, along with another frying pan of a half dozen lovely fried eggs. My own system was to quickly cut up my meat, break two biscuits into four halves, cover all this with gravy, then place three eggs on top. I would break the yokes so the yellow part mixed with all the rest and it just seemed like I couldn't get it into my mouth fast enough. The taste was so good, I can still vividly remember it today. Once Mr. Jackson said, "That boy will eat us out of house and home." I went cold all over with fear; but when I looked at Mrs. Jackson, she was smiling her little smile, so I guess he was kidding.

Above the table was a shelf with some painted plates on it, along with Mr. Jackson's Bible. It was a big Bible; and I knew he would take it down and read a page before we ate. Mr. Jackson hardly ever talked to me; but sometimes, when he finished reading the Bible and after saying the blessing, he would ask me if I understood what he had read. When I first came I would say I didn't; but now I wanted him to like me and be proud of my learning to milk and do the other work, so I would ask questions, and sometimes we talked. This was the only time we really talked to each other, and I liked this very much. Mrs. Jackson didn't say much either; but I thought she liked me a little bit. She knew I was practically starving to death; and sometimes when she filled my plate, I could see her smile just a little. I always watched closely, hoping she would smile.

This morning Mr. Jackson read the Bible as usual. His method of reading the Bible was to start at the beginning and read a page or two each day until the whole Bible was read; then he would start over. I had learned much of the Bible because of this, and also from asking questions so Mr. Jackson would talk to me. This morning he read from the Chapter of Saint Luke. It was something about a good tree not bringing forth corrupt fruit, neither could a corrupt tree bring forth good fruit. Then he read some more and it was something like, A good man out of the good treasure of his heart brings forth that which is good and an evil man brings forth that which is evil. As he finished reading this, he suddenly closed the Bible and

before I could even ask a question, he got up and went outside. I was
surprised because he usually liked to discuss what had been read.

After eating, I just had time to catch the school bus. I had now been
with the Jacksons for two years and I was starting my freshman year in high
school. The bus came to the end of our lane, then took us about eight
miles into the small town where the high school was located. It was not
really a school bus like some of the other kids rode. This was a small truck
with a canvas top over it and inside a bench down each side for us to sit
on. There were eight of us who rode in this bus and I was the third one to
be picked up. Two of the kids lived close to town; so they sometimes
walked. We would usually pass them just as they were getting to school,
and always yelled and hollered as we went by. They would yell and wave
and start to run after us, but the bus driver wouldn't stop; and they would
have to walk all the way in. Sometimes I wished I could get off and walk
with them.

The high school was built from red brick and had ten classrooms, a study
hall and a gymnasium. The first day I came to school I was lost and scared.
At the home, we had all gone to the same school, so I knew the other kids;
and we had our own group. We were known as the "home kids"; and even
though we wished the other kids would let us play or join them, if they
didn't we still had each other. In this school, I was all alone, and scared
because I didn't know anybody. I even got mixed up on my rooms, when
the bell rang to change classes, and I ended up out in the hall by myself.
All the doors to the rooms were closed, and I was too frightened to open
any of them and ask where to go, so I just stood there feeling sick and
lonely, until I began to cry.

The principal's name was Mr. Beattie; and I don't know what I would
have done if he hadn't come out of his office, and found me standing there.
He took me in his office, closed the door and sat there quietly while I cried
and cried, as though I couldn't stop. When I finally did stop I felt much
better; and he and I went down to the boy's bathroom so I could wash my

face. I liked him very much and he told me to come to see him if I needed any help. Sometimes when I saw him in the hall he would nod or smile, and since I didn't think he did this to all the other boys, I felt pretty proud about it.

My classes were difficult. I was taking English, history, algebra and literature. Literature was my favorite. I liked to read stories, *The Lady of the Lake* and *King Arthur's Knights of The Round Table*, because the main characters seemed to have a such a great time. Sometimes I would dream about them, while sitting with my friend, the stove instead of thinking about having my own home. We would rescue fair maidens in distress, fight dragons; and I would always win the jousting tournaments.

The final bell would ring about four o'clock and I didn't dare miss the bus home. Many of the boys stayed to play basketball, but I had to get home, load the wagon with hay, and help milk. It would be almost dark when we finished our chores. I would study for awhile and then maybe get to read about Sir Lancelot. He was my favorite of all King Arthur's Knights. If I could read about him tonight before I went to bed, maybe he would let me ride with him for awhile in the morning. Of course he would have to wait until I got a fire going in the stove.

So the winter passed day after day with very little change. School was easier and more fun since I had gotten acquainted with some of the other kids and had made friends. One boy, especially, had become a close friend. His name was Rodney and he lived about a mile from me. Sometimes on a Saturday, if the work was finished, Mr. Jackson would let me go over to his house to visit. Rod was the oldest of three children; and he had one brother and one sister.

Rod's sister, Ellen, was one year younger than I; and she was very pretty. She had long blond hair; and she seemed to love to tease me, causing me to get tongue-tied and embarrassed. Each time before going over to their house I thought that I would act differently, and would be witty or say something intelligent, but I never did; and it always ended up the same way, with me red faced and speechless.

One of the big events in the community was the box social, which was held at the local Grange Hall each year. I had never heard of one before; but Rod said the women and girls filled a shoe box with fried chicken, cake and other good food, wrote their name on the outside of the box, and put it on a table to be auctioned off. The auctioneer called out the girl's name that was on the box, and started the bidding. Sometimes, if two or three boys wanted to buy a certain girl's shoe box, Rod told me the bid could get up to as high as a dollar and fifty cents. Mr. Jackson gave me twenty-five cents a week as an allowance; and I had saved two dollars and twenty five cents. My mind was already made up that I would bid it all, if necessary, to be with Ellen. The successful bidder would get to sit with the girl and they would eat the food together. If I were willing to pay this much, it should impress her, and make me look good in her eyes.

I thought about her a lot in the mornings now, along with Sir Lancelot. I didn't understand this, because I never thought anybody would take his place. But Sir Lancelot had never made me feel warm all over with a tingling pleasant sensation in my stomach, like thinking about Ellen did.

The box supper was this next Saturday night, and since all the farmers belonged to the Grange, Mr. and Mrs. Jackson were going so I would get to go also. By Saturday night I was so nervous that when we finally got there, it was hard to sit still. Rod and I were sitting together with some other boys, with all the girls in a group giggling and whispering, and sneaking a glance at us to see if we were watching.

Ellen was with them and was wearing a yellow dress with a matching yellow ribbon in her hair. With her blue eyes and the yellow dress, she seemed to me to be the most beautiful thing in the world. As I watched her I was caught up in my day dreams again; and almost missed getting a chance to bid when her name was called. Rod told me later that the bid was going for sixty cents when he jabbed me in the ribs. I jumped up and said two dollars and twenty five cents in a loud voice, which caused everyone to

look at me, and laugh. It was worth it though because after we had sat
together and eaten, during which time I still couldn't be witty or wise, Ellen
put her hand in mine and led me outside. People were getting ready to
leave, but in the dark by the corner of the Grange Hall Ellen put her arms
around my waist and kissed me. From that moment on Sir Lancelot was
gone forever.

School was finally out and we were well into the summer's work. The
cows still had to be milked every morning and night and the long hot
summer days in between were spent irrigating; or cutting, raking and
stacking the alfalfa hay, as it got ready. The first cutting was done and we
were just starting the second. I spent hours sitting on a mowing machine
which was pulled by two horses; then more hours sitting on a buck rake.
The buck rake was ten feet wide with several curved tines that rested on the
ground. After the mowed alfalfa hay had dried enough, the buck rake
would rake it into rows across the field. The rake had a trip that was kicked
to keep the rows in a continuous line. Then the rake would go down the
length of the rows, so that the hay was in shocks, ready to be pitched up
onto the hay wagon. The team and wagon went between these shocks,
with a man on each side, throwing the hay onto the wagon with pitchforks.
My job was to drive the hay wagon. The horses were wise and had done
this work so many times, that they would stay between the rows, without
any guiding. I would tie the reins to what was called a Jacobs ladder, which
was actually a ladder fastened to the front of the hay wagon, so it was
possible to climb up or down from a full load of hay.

As the hay was pitched onto the wagon I spread it evenly and tramped it
down, until the load was as high as the men with the pitchforks could
reach. Then I drove the wagon to the stack and unloaded it, with a
mormon derrick and a jackson fork. I asked one of the neighbors if Mr.
Jackson had invented the jackson fork, and he laughed and said, "No, I
don't think so". Later I heard him repeating my question to the other men
and they all laughed, but I didn't understand why they thought it was so
funny.

A Mormon derrick with a Jackson fork.

The derrick had a long pole almost sixty feet long with the center of the pole mounted on the peak of a frame, twenty five feet from the ground. The Jackson fork was about five feet wide with six long curved tines. These tines were fastened to a solid oak frame and held in a curved position by a catch. This catch had a place to attach a long rope. When I drove the wagon to the hay stack, the fork was lowered to the load and I would firmly force it into the hay on the wagon. Another man would lead a good steady horse to lift the loaded Jackson fork up and over the stack, where the stacker could position it over the place he wanted it dumped, and holler "Trip!". I would pull the rope, release the catch and continue to do this until the wagon was unloaded, then head back to the field for another load. All of it was hard work, with the hot sun causing the sweat to run off you in streams. The hard work and the sweat mixed with the inescapable hay dust leaves you itching and worn out by the end of the day.

After we would finish for the day, I always went down behind the barn, out of sight, stripped off all my clothes and stood naked in the cool water of the pond trying to wash the dust off. One evening Ellen and her parents came over to see Mr. and Mrs. Jackson, but Ellen stayed outside. I was standing in the pond, busily washing myself, when I looked up and there she stood watching me. She must have been standing there for quite awhile without my knowing it. I was so shocked I couldn't move and just stood there. Then without any real conscious thought on my part, I began to get the strangest feeling between my legs. She gazed at this while time stood still for me; then with a small strange smile that showed just a flash of her teeth, she turned and was gone.

Most of the haying was done by the farmers themselves. They would all gather at each others' farms with their teams and wagons and share the work until the haying was finished. Strict unwritten rules were followed. One man would owe two days haying or another three which was determined by the number of days a person had helped his neighbor. This was a man's word and was always settled before the end of the summer. If extra help was needed and the farmer would have to hire men. The standard pay for a hay hand was $2.00 a day. A good stacker was a professional in every sense of the word and could demand up to $5.00 a day. How a stack was trampled down and shaped to shed rain and snow was very important, and if the sides were not straight and square the stack could actually fall over.

A mainline railroad track ran near the farm, with a section of track called a siding, built along side of it. Often long freight trains pulled onto this siding and stood panting noisily so another train could go by. Next to these tracks was a small stream of water with lots of willows and a few other trees growing along its banks. The many men who rode these trains were called bindle stiffs or hobos.

Since the stream was there and there was plenty of wood for fires, it was an ideal place for these men to stay for a day or two. Sometimes one of them came to the house and asked for something to eat; and if Mr. Jackson weren't around Mrs. Jackson always found something to give them. The men had some mysterious way of knowing when Mr. Jackson was gone, because they never came to the house when he was home. Mr. Jackson had told me never to go around the siding. He talked about things these men would do to a boy, none of which I understood, but he seemed to be very concerned about it and cautioned me over and over again. The way he looked at me and the change in the tone of his voice was enough to keep me away from the siding. This was where a farmer would go if he needed to hire extra help.

Most of the hobos didn't want a job haying, but usually one or two would decide to work for a few days. They would get two dollars a day, plus board. I think the food was more of an inducement than the money. There were no better cooks in the world than two or three farm women in a kitchen during haying time; and the hobos knew it. All the farmers tried to get the younger men because they were healthy and strong and could pitch hay all day long without stopping. Some of them were not much older than I; and when they stripped off their shirts and pitched the hay up to me on the wagon, I could look down at their bare shoulders and watch their muscles rippling under a sheen of sweat.

Almost none of them would ever work for Mr. Jackson. He would go to the siding quite often, and would be gone for two or three hours sometimes, even when he really didn't need any help. Once in awhile an old man would come back with him and drive the stacker team; but he just didn't have any luck hiring the younger men. I didn't know why because Mrs. Jackson was a very good cook.

Sometimes I would think about leaving here and the thought would fill me with excitement. Even though I had been warned to stay away from the siding, I had listened to the young men lying around in the shade, talking about the places they had gone and the things they had done. They talked about working in the mines and some of them had sawed timber. Others worked just enough to eat, drifting south in the winter and up north during the summer. They all seemed free and independent; and they laughed a lot. At night, when I laid in bed, I was filled with a strange longing. The steam whistles on the trains rushing by in the night had long mournful wails, and a lonely compelling sound that seemed to say, "Come along with me e e e e e, Come along with me e e e e e.!"

I was also disturbed by other urges that I didn't understand; something strange had happened to my body. Almost every night now, in spite of anything else, the image of Ellen standing and looking at me while I was in the pond would come back and I would find myself rubbing the place where I got that first strange sensation. For a long time I have hidden a towel beside my bed and each night I barely reach it in time before I am relieved. Once the towel was gone and I knew Mrs. Jackson must have found it. I wondered what she thought and wished I could ask her what was happening to me. I saw the same towel later, washed and put away but she never said a word. I felt ashamed and didn't know why and yet I could never go to sleep until it happened.

Last night while I was asleep I heard something in my room. I woke up and could just barely make out Mr. Jackson standing over my bed. The pale light from the moon was shining through the window and made strange patterns on the quilt and across his body. He didn't say anything; but just stood there looking down at me. Suddenly he reached down and pulled all the covers off me leaving me lying there on my back. I was sure I was going to be pulled out of bed, but instead he dropped to his knees at the side of the bed and buried his face against my stomach. I thought he was sick and I was just getting ready to call to Mrs. Jackson for help, when I heard her voice, calling his name. I was sure he must have been sick because he gave a kind of wrenching sob and left. I pulled the covers back over me and lay there for awhile wondering if he was all right. But I didn't hear another sound and soon went back to sleep.

When I woke up at the usual time, and went downstairs, I found Mr. and Mrs. Jackson sitting at the kitchen table. There was already a fire going in the stove, and the coffee was made. They had evidently been up for some time. This was very strange and it was the first time it had ever happened since I had come to live with them. Mrs. Jackson must have been crying for a long time because her face was tear streaked and her eyes were red. She got up from the table when I came in, looked at me silently for a moment, then turned and went upstairs. I sat there with my first feelings of concern, knowing something was terribly wrong. I heard her cross the floor to her bed and lie down, then heard the faint sounds of her crying. It had a haunting helpless note to it and reminded me of the lonely sadness that the train whistles made in the night. Mr. Jackson was listening also and his face was filled with despair.

All my hopes of finally having a home and family of my own were finished as he attempted to explain to me the desires with which he was cursed. He explained his affliction in terms of God and the Devil. He explained that with fervent prayers and strength he had fought this terrible urge and usually won; but occasionally his resolve weakened and the Devil entered his mind and body, and he did these loathsome acts.

I didn't really know or understand all of the things he was saying; but I did understand it was done with another man or preferably with a boy. As I listened to him talk, I began to be filled with hurt and disillusionment. Hurt because I had yearned so desperately for a home and for love; disillusionment because I had given him my complete trust hoping that this had finally come true. He went on talking about God punishing him for his sins; and then he started to cry, got down his Bible and began to pray. I sat there and watched this man I had practically idolized, weeping and praying; and I watched him with a surprising new awareness, as though it were someone else and not I, witnessing this destruction of my trust. Then this other person was filled with a cold sense of determination that he would never again believe in anything or anybody, to the point of being hurt. Even the Bible laying there, took on new meaning. As his lips moved over it I could feel them again on my bare stomach and the association of the two would never leave me.

Mr. Jackson had now forgotten me as he prayed and cried in this strange world of his own making. My new self was looking around and wondering what I was doing there. The plates on the shelf were dingy, and I smiled as I looked at that monstrous stove sitting there, realizing how childish it had been to sit in front of it dreaming of anything. Almost in a panic I knew that I must leave this place, so I turned and ran up to my room.

One time Rod had given me an old Indian blanket when I was over at his house. It had an assorted interlaced pattern of design that I had admired, and even though it was old and the colors had long since faded, it was one of my most prized possessions; probably because he had just given it to me for no particular reason.

I was beginning to feel a mounting excitement as I gathered the things I planned to take, an extra pair of jeans, a shirt and some socks. It could all be rolled up in the blanket quite easily. I found a piece of clothes line to tie it with and had a bedroll made just like all the hobos carried. A loop of the clothes line went across my shoulders so that my hands would be left free. This was called a bindle. Adjusting this loop just right I was a little proud of my new role. I had just become a bindle stiff.

Mrs. Jackson's door was closed; and I hesitated briefly, considering whether to tell her goodbye or to just leave. I will always be grateful for the impulse that caused me to knock on her door and go in. She had stopped crying and was just lying there with her eyes open staring at the ceiling.

I have thought of her many times, of the sorrow she suffered in not having any children and of the terrible burden of guilt she was forced to share, through no fault of her own. What final pain she must have felt as she saw me standing by her bed with my bedroll, knowing I was leaving her also. The tears ran from her eyes again as she reached her arms toward me; and I knelt down beside the bed and laid my cheek next to that helpless wet one. She clung to me with a fierce intensity which I accepted with an infinite wisdom of understanding far beyond my years. I truly gave of myself, unselfishly giving her the only gesture of acceptance and love she might have ever felt.

Finally I took her arms away and without empty words turned and left. This picture comes back to me often when I think of her, along with the memory of the small smile she would give me when she filled my plate. I have always been thankful that I took the time to say goodbye to her

Her sorrow was still in my mind when I went downstairs. Mr. Jackson was still sitting over his Bible, his face ravaged and swollen from his weeping and praying. A strange thing happened as we silently looked at each other. I felt like I was the adult and he was the child. Also I felt a terrible contempt in my heart. I thought he was a hypocrite, with his tears dripping on his Bible which I knew would never wash away the sins he had committed. The lifetime of sorrow he had caused that other person upstairs and his weakness of the flesh could not be justified with his words about God. And me, what had he done to me, as he destroyed my dreams and yearnings as a child. I wondered if I would ever be able to believe in anything again.

All of this went through my mind in the small interval of time that I stood there; and suddenly, it seemed as though he could see the things I was thinking and could see them to be true. The realization of the things he would have to face on judgment day caused his face to pale with awareness and fear. That was the way I left him as I turned and went out the door.

When I walked out of the Jacksons' house, I had just started my second year of high school; but, what with getting up early and having to get home to load hay and milk, it had been no fun. I was quick with good reaction times and I would have loved to play football and basketball in high school, but couldn't because of the farm chores.

Also, I remember being chased by eight or ten boys who were throwing snowballs. I finally just sat down, turned my back, and put my head on my arms. I realize now that children can be the cruelest creatures on earth, especially if they sense a weak or dysfunctional child. They will tease him unmercifully as they did me; so I had no regrets in leaving school either, as I walked away from my childhood.

CHAPTER 2
THE BEGINNING

My steps quickened with excitement as I hurried toward the siding. I felt that out there someplace might be the answers to some of my questions so I must hasten if I intended to find them. A long freight train was waiting and I imagined the engine looked like a mighty horse covered with black trappings. The wheels would strike sparks from the rails like his steel shod hooves striking the cobblestones, and the escaping steam looked like snorting breath from red flared nostrils. The engine whistle sounded like shrill neighing. It was an impatient calling; and Sir Lancelot and I were ready. He was the only companion I wanted as I left the hope of my childhood dreams behind me forever.

One of the young men who had worked with me in the hay was at the siding when I arrived. He looked at me and my bindle and asked if I was running away. When I said, " I guess I am," it didn't seem to surprise him and he gestured for me to follow him. He and I and four other men climbed in the open door of a box car. The first thing they did was wedge the door open. The young man explained that sometimes the door was closed and locked from the outside. If anyone was trapped inside they could ride for hundreds of miles or the car could be set aside on a siding and stand for days. Then they started telling stories about getting trapped and described in gruesome detail what agonies of thirst and hunger these poor men had suffered. One told about a man who had tried to claw his way out with his fingernails; and when they found his body the bones of his fingers were splintered and the flesh was stripped from his hands.

Another told of three men being trapped, all finally dying; but before they did the last one alive had begun to eat from the bodies of the other two. This was told with grim humor and the guy finished by saying that two of the men had been big and strong while the one who had lived the longest was about my size. My teachers in school had had a hard time getting lessons through my head, probably because I didn't pay attention; but these teachers were having much better luck.

At first, with the excitement of leaving, and listening to these stories, I was sure I would never sleep; but I rolled my blanket out on the floor, took off my shoes and lay down. The floor was hard and shook from vibration, but the rhythmic sound of the wheels as they crossed each rail joint created a strange rhythm that could almost be set to music. So with this, my first lullaby, I went to sleep. We traveled fast but slowed down while going through one of the many small towns. Sometimes we stopped; and I was aware of movement around me in the darkness of the car, and knew that some of the men I started with had left, and others had taken their place. After a stop and in order to get the train moving again, the engineer would spin the engine's wheels quickly jerking the first eight or ten cars into movement to take up the slack. Then he would slow down, but the chain reaction set up by the first cars would be felt coming down the line of boxcars, until it reached ours. I could hear it coming but I was always startled, when suddenly our car would feel as though a giant hammer had knocked it completely off the tracks. Then I would hear profound curses from the men in the dark around me. Their description of the engineer when this would happen would be given in very clear convincing tones of voice, leaving no doubt in my mind that they were right. Sometime during the night, when it happened again, I added my meager contribution to the others; and it could very well have been just enough to consign the engineer to hell forever. Anyway, I was surprised at how pleased I was with myself.

It must have been five o'clock in the morning because I was wide awake, ready to go milk. It took a few minutes to realize where I was and I laid there thinking about all the things that had happened. It was the first time I have had time to remember, and I didn't seem to feel any regrets. I was filled with guilty pleasurable relief, knowing no one would call me to get up; and that I am as free as a bird. I had no idea where I was but I lay there thinking, listening to the wheels and seeing the lights flash by in the darkness. My black charger out in front blasted his scream of defiance into the night.

As daylight entered the car I was able to see about me. There were only two other men left in the car besides me and they were not the same ones who had started out with me. Also, my shoes were gone. I felt a sense of loss when I saw that the young man was gone too; he was my last link with home. Now the separation seems to be final and complete. It was probably not true, but in my mind, I thought that he was the one who had stolen my shoes. Suddenly, I experienced some fears and doubts about having left home.

Losing my shoes was quite a shock. I had gone to church regularly for the past year, and had sat in a Sunday school class, listening to a preacher tell about the love each man should feel for his brother. He had not prepared me for this. The preacher had created a dream world of fantasy for his flock to share. Some of the older people in the congregation who listened, must have clung to the hope that life could be the way he described it. Having long before suspected, as I have now found out the true reality, the preacher must be living out a lifetime of hypocrisy and pretense. He asked people to cover up all natural base motives, suppress hidden desires with righteousness, and go back once each week to reinforce their doubts with another dose.

It all seemed so simple. God had given me the power to reason. I had not reasoned but instead had taken off my shoes and left them lying there in the dark among strangers. One of these strangers needed shoes and had taken mine. Of course I hadn't wanted to lose my shoes, yet I gave a mental nod of acceptance to this new realization; and I could almost see that it was a cheap price to pay, because now I was starting to think.

One of the other things I thought about was my stomach. It was way past my usual biscuits and gravy time and I was getting very hungry. The train was slowing down for another town and when it finally stopped I gingerly eased myself down to the sharp rocks and cinders along the track. The train didn't stay long and Blackie gave me two short farewell whistles before pulling away, leaving me standing there.

Now the full realization of what I had done descended upon me. I felt a wave of self pity come over my whole body. Here I was barefooted, a little cold and very hungry. I was just a kid and yet I was standing here in this strange place with no one in the whole world who knew how lonely I was and worst of all, didn't care. What a dejected figure I must have made, feeling as I did, while, I made my slow barefoot way toward the town.

It was a small town. There were probably thousands like it across the country: with one main street, a dry goods store, a grocery store and two pool halls. Each business was barely making a living and competing for the few dollars available to be spent. This early in the morning nothing was open except the one restaurant. As I approached it, the smell of cooking food was more than I could stand, and I knew I must have something to eat.

The name on the door said Maud's Café, and as I opened it and went in, a woman came out of the kitchen. She was a fairly tall, well-built woman about middle age. Her black hair was just beginning to show streaks of gray along the sides. Her face must have once been very pretty, but now seemed more old and tired than it should have been.

The café was empty and we stood there looking at each other. The sight of men carrying a bedroll was a common and ordinary sight in any town, especially one like this, next to a railroad. She must have either fed or turned away many men while running a restaurant. She may have even turned me away, except that in spite of all my new found bravado and self reliance, my self-pity was too much and two large tears ran down my cheeks. I hated myself for it but I couldn't help it; and I guess those tears making streaks through the train smoke on my face, along with my bare feet were more than she could take. Her face softened as I stood there in mute appeal and she told me to go into the restroom and wash my face and hands. When I came out there was a stack of hot cakes and a glass of milk ready for me to eat. How deliciously good they were! I forgot any table manners I might have learned and gobbled them down in a hurry.

While I was eating Maud was watching and when I finished she asked me if I would like to stay. She told me she was a widow who had lost her husband four years ago in a mining accident. With her husband's insurance she had bought this café, had been running it alone, but was getting tired from all the work and needed help.

She lived upstairs by herself and went on to say that if I stayed, there was another room that could be fixed up for me to sleep in. In return I would wash dishes, clean up the tables and sweep floors. If I would do this acceptably, then I could have a bed and all the food I wanted to eat. The mention of more food made the decision pretty easy.

The room she gave me was large and warm; and I liked it. I broke the habit of getting up at five o'clock and now didn't have to get up until six. Plus the restaurant had a restroom inside, so I felt my lot in life had improved a great deal.

My first job of the day was still to build a fire in the huge cook stove and put water on for coffee. I thoroughly enjoyed working in the kitchen. It was warm and cozy, and filled with the smell of Maud's cooking. She bustled efficiently back and forth during the busy times carrying food one way and the dirty dishes the other. These I washed in hot soapy suds up to my elbows.

After the rush was over we would spend many pleasant hours sitting at one of the tables talking, with Maud occasionally having to get up to wait on a customer. We discussed many things and I found that she had a simple unshakable belief in religion. I had learned quite a few teachings from the Bible and would argue with her that these teachings were contradictory to the real facts of life. When I thought that I had her convinced with my arguments she would just smile and say, "You should have more faith." What can you say to a statement like that?

Many men came to the kitchen door asking for food; and since it was winter now, they were cold with their faces pinched from despair and hunger. They all began to look the same to me, a continual stream of human faces with no identity. I thought that some of them must have had money and could have bought something to eat if they wanted to, but whenever there was food left over Maud gave it away. I argued with her about this, but she would say "Jesus broke the bread, took the fishes and fed the multitude". It did no good for me to point out that Jesus could perform miracles and she couldn't; or that He had a damn sight more backing than she did; but I guess she must have felt the backing was the same.

She taught Sunday school each Sunday and always tried to get me to go to church with her. I didn't even try to explain why I wouldn't go. I had been there almost three months and today was my birthday. I was sixteen years old and I thought I was a man. I told Maud that it was my birthday, so she baked me a cake. After the café was closed for the day we sat in the kitchen to eat it. It was a beautiful cake with sixteen candles on it. Maud lit the candles, sang "Happy Birthday" and told me to make a wish before I blew the candles out. When she asked, "What did you wish for", I told her, "I wished that I could stay here forever". This made her sad and she started talking about her husband, and went to get a picture of him to show me. It was a picture of a tall good-looking man with black hair and a black mustache.

I made some remark about the mustache and she laughed and said how it had tickled when he had kissed her. Then she became very quiet for a moment while looking at the picture, and started to cry.

I didn't know what to do but I went to her, put my hands on her shoulders, and quietly said, "Please don't cry, everything will be all right." Suddenly she stood up, put her arms around me and clung to me tightly with a fierce, surprising strength. I just stood there, helplessly holding her, when that strange sensation started happening to me again. I was embarrassed and tried to step back but she had felt it too. She looked into my face, then took my hand and led me upstairs to her room. With a strange detached fascination I stood there and watched as she took off all her clothes.

Then completely naked she came to me and started to unbutton my shirt. At the touch of her fingers I was filled with a wild uncontrollable excitement. On the farm a neighbor used to bring his stud to breed with the mares. The stud would paw and snort and almost go crazy until he could ram himself into the mare. Visions of this, of Ellen and of lurid dreams, all flashed together in a jumbled picture in my mind. I was shaking so badly that Maud had to unbutton my pants also. Then she pulled me down with her on the bed. What a terrible urgency and need I had. I spent myself frantically four or five times, sometimes in her, more often on her until I finally laid there in a sweaty, sticky exhaustion. During all this time she had passively laid there, holding me tightly in her arms when I burst, and murmuring soothingly in between times. How wonderful it was and how beautiful she looked. Her face was serene and she was smiling like the Madonna does in the picture.

She had learned to live with desire and had long since filed it away along with the memories of her husband. This kind and generous person gave me food and shelter and finally her body to help me during my time of need. I'd like to think it was mutual, but I'm not so sure. Even during our many times together as she taught me gentleness and consideration in the act of love, I always felt that she was doing it for the same reasons that she gave away food.

I wondered sometimes which teaching from the Bible she used to justify her behavior.

As for me I felt very fortunate that my first was with this quiet and experienced woman. Being past the wild passion of youth she taught me that making love could be like making music. Gently touching the right keys creates a symphony of pleasure. Striking them too hard destroys the music and spoils the effect.

What a long winter it was The ground had not been seen since early last fall because of the snow. Temperatures had stayed low and Maud mentioned that the snow depth and extreme cold had broken records going back for many years. None of this bothered me very much because I seldom went outside. If I did go out, it was to take a short walk to one of the pool halls across the street. There were only two of them, both about the same in looks. They smelled exactly the same inside; the odor of stale beer mixed with tobacco smoke. The men who sat there day after day looked the same too and would divide their sitting time equally between the two places. Some were older and retired, getting small pensions from the companies where they had spent the better part of their lives. Others had worked during the summer, either on farms or on logging jobs, saving part of their summer's wages and along with the new unemployment compensation program, managed to get by until work opened up again in the spring.

Usually they would all start drifting in around ten o'clock, buy a ten cent glass of beer nursing it at one of the tables. This was the pattern of their lives; some had given a lifetime of service to this, others were still in the process.

I would sit and watch different ones and speculated about their lives. I wondered what hopes and dreams they had had in their youths. Or, I wondered, did they ever have a purpose or expect anything even in the beginning? Could a whole life be lived without purpose; or end up without a purpose and if so was there any sustaining feature? If there were such a feature I couldn't see it in them. It looked to me like man's inhumane trapping of man with the bait having many guises: job security, company loyalty, advancement, and the best bait of all, a pension. Some of these men had given forty years of their lives for this bait, not knowing that the trap had slammed shut on their body and soul, twenty years before. They had gotten to this point, by tasting the bait, only to find that it was spoiled.

Occasionally one of the older men would die. After he died all the rest of the men would attend his funeral. I went once but never again. The preacher talked at great length about the exemplary life this man had lived; how good he had been; and how much he had loved the great outdoors and his fellow man. The preacher created a word picture of him that did not fit my picture of him. I remembered him sitting at one of the tables in a dirty pool hall, with clothes worn and his old overcoat held together with a safety pin. His rheumy eyes would look vacantly through the wisps of gray hair that hung over them. As the preacher went on about his life, I could see the old man sitting there trying to take another sip of beer, with hands that trembled so badly that part of the beer ran out the corners of his mouth, dripping unknowingly from his chin onto his coat The preacher went on to say that now the old man had gone home, to a place where the streets were paved with gold and angels sang, where everyone was happy, never again to be cold or hungry.

As I listened, and watched his friends sitting there waiting their turn to get a chance at Heaven, I wondered why, if all this were true, they couldn't have had a small share of it during their life time on earth. If the preacher were right a little of that abundance would never have been missed. A good, just God should have known that. One practical thing I would have asked for the old man was: "Please steady his hand when he drinks his beer, he has worked so very hard all his life for that dime."

After I had been there awhile, Maud encouraged me to go back to school. She said that I could help her in the mornings and evenings, because weekends were the busiest times anyway. But I didn't want to go. The horrors of trying to understand algebra were still fresh in my mind.

One of the customers who came into the café was named Jack Catapolis. He was from a Greek family in town and was about my age. Jack had Greek features and coloring, with dark skin and jet black hair. He had let his hair grow long on the sides and on his neck and looked very handsome. At least the girls thought so. There was a high school in the town and occasionally Jack brought in one of the high school girls for ice cream or a coke.

I did miss kids my own age and got to know a few of them, like Jack after they came into the café a few times. Jack was on the football team and with his looks, he seemed to have had his pick of any girl in the school. He came in with a different girl each time and all of them were very pretty. Whenever he would come in alone I would get us a couple of cokes and we would sit at a table and talk. Mostly he talked and I listened. He talked about school, the trouble he was having with one class or another, how dumb some of his teachers were and about girls.

Girls seemed to be the subject he liked best and knew the most about. To hear him tell it this was one place where he didn't neglect his homework. He bragged about his conquests and I was surprised at the number of different ones he claimed to have had. If one of his conquests came in, I would look at her and wonder if she had actually given in to him or if he were just lying. He told about one girl in particular, named Mary, describing in lurid detail just what had taken place and how she had acted. She was a blond and ever since Ellen, blondes have had just a little preference when I thought about girls. Mary even looked a little like Ellen.

The next time Jack came in I asked him if he would fix it so I could take her on a date "Sure," he said, "I'll get everything lined up." The next day he came in and said it was all set. He had a car and we planned to double date this coming Saturday night. We decided to go to a show in one of the neighboring towns. When I told Maud what we had planned she seemed quite pleased that I was getting out with someone my own age. She gave me three dollars so that I had money for our tickets and refreshments.

Everything went off as planned. I got all slicked up, spending an hour on my hair alone, and Jack picked me up right on time. I got into the back seat with Mary and off we went. The show was good but I couldn't concentrate on it too much because I was thinking about Mary and how I would surprise her with all my newly learned techniques in making love. Little did she realize as she sat there what wonderful pleasures were in store for her.

After the show we went to a drive-in for a hamburger and a milkshake. I was getting more impatient all the time and wondered why Jack wasn't as anxious as I was to get down to the main purpose of the evening. But he didn't seem to be in any hurry so we just sat there talking about the show. Finally we were in the car headed toward home and I could start my brilliant maneuvers. First, I slid next to Mary putting my arm around her shoulders, which seemed fine with her, as she snuggled up and put her head on my shoulder.

This left my right hand free and I began to softly stroke her hair, then gradually let my fingers trail across the hollow of her neck. She was wearing a dress that wasn't really low cut but left part of her upper bosom exposed. I bent over and kissed her there, expecting to find her beginning to tingle with anticipation. She just sat there, not resisting but certainly not going wild with passion, either. Thinking that maybe she was past these childish antics, I reached down and ran my hand up the inside of her leg to her crotch. After that I don't know what happened. She let out a screech that could have been heard a mile away, causing Jack and his date to jump a foot, with Jack damn near running off the road. At the same time Mary was continuing to shriek, started to cry, and told Jack to take her home. She sat clear over in the corner of the back seat and cried all the way to her house.

As soon as Jack stopped the car she jumped out and ran inside. Jack took me back to the café with no one saying a word. I guess we were all in a state of shock. I know I was. How could this have happened to such a great lover as I?

The next day I was bent over the sink washing dishes when I heard someone come into the café. I never gave it a thought until suddenly I was jerked almost off my feet and slammed against the kitchen wall. It seemed that Mary had run sobbing into her house, found her parents still up, and told them what I had done. Mary's mother had gone into hysterics, finally needing a sedative to quiet her down, and insisted the next morning that Mary be given a physical examination, which proved her virginity was still intact.

It was Mary's father who had grabbed me and was now standing there, white faced, and shaking with rage. I was very frightened; and even though he was so upset that he could hardly talk; I understood that if I didn't leave town immediately, not only would he beat me to death, but he would also have me arrested for attempted rape. At the time I didn't realize he couldn't do both at the same time, and I was thoroughly convinced he had meant just what he said.

I felt a moment of regret about this turn or events. Not so much in having to leave, because it was time to go anyway, but in thinking about the reasons behind my having to leave. My first experiences with Maud had led me to believe that sex was something that could be given with gentleness and compassion. The one place in all the misery of life where two people could share in the honest joy of giving, simply for each other's pleasure. I thought of it as a small island of time when minds and bodies were at peace. Now I found that this belief was not so.

Poor Mary, throughout the rest of her life I doubt if she ever found the island. We had our time of sadness, Maud and I, as she helped me get my things ready to leave. She had been a lonely woman and I had been a lonely kid. And I have come to believe that there was a destiny that brought us together. Our coming together for this short time, filled a loneliness created when her husband died and in an unusual way perhaps I took the place of the child she never had.

In all of this I learned from her that love can stand without apology on its own, without mumbled man-made words of hypocrisy needed to sanction it. If peace in a person's heart can only come from God; then who on earth can condemn it, when you find this peace, regardless of how or where it is found.

CHAPTER 3
LESSONS FOR SURVIVAL

LIFE'S STRUGGLE

Ah, you insignificant worm.
You thing of human form
Struggling to survive
in relation to the universe.
Your mind becomes a curse
forcing you to squirm
among all other things alive.

Theirs are dictated by instinct.
Yours, because you supposedly think.
Yet they seem to simply survive
while you struggle to stay alive.
Both do live and both do die.
But only man is forced to cry.

The railroad companies did not provide empty boxcars just for the convenience of the vast numbers of men who traveled from one place to another. While there were generally empty cars going each way, and even though it didn't cost them anything extra, they did everything possible to prevent men from riding in them. Every railroad town of any size had big tough men hired to keep the hobos off the trains.

These men worked for the railroad and were given an almost free hand to deal with the hobos in their own way. These railroad bulls, as they were called, carried guns and a heavy night stick, either of which they did not hesitate to use, if necessary. Some seemed to become sadists with the power they held over less fortunate men. Occasionally one of the railroad bulls was found dead, especially if he had gotten the reputation of being unreasonably mean. Their reputation was known by hobos from one end of the country to the other. This special information was shared by the network of riding hobos and was reliable and efficient.. With a piece of chalk, full details were given on the inside walls of the cars. It covered a variety of subjects such as, "Watch the bastard in such and such a town, he's a killer," or avoid such and such because of a road project underway which would utilize free labor by arresting everyone for vagrancy, and sentencing them to thirty days to six months on a labor gang. Even the good and bad jails were listed. This information was very important and saved many a man from trouble, allowing him to drop off at the edge of town as the train slowed down instead of riding into the yards and either being beaten or sentenced to some form of captive labor. I had gotten to know the two railroad bulls since they always ate at Maud's Cafe They didn't seem to be quite as bad as the ones I had heard of in other towns, yet their jobs depended on them doing what they had been hired to do. Even so, having listened to them talk about some of the pitiful sights they had seen, I suspected that they occasionally risked their jobs to give someone a break. One of the yard bulls came into the café just as I was getting ready to leave and spent some ten minutes back in the kitchen talking to Maud. Then he and Maud came over to where I was sitting at one of the tables. Maud had a soft determined look on her face, so I suspected someone was either hungry or needed help. What I didn't know was how much I was to become involved in the story they told.

The bull told me that a young married woman about twenty eight years old had been found in one of the cars on the train that had just pulled in. The woman was cold and half starved, but the worst part of all was that she had three small children with her. Her husband had left their home some six months ago seeking work. After he found a job he would send money home each month for food but there just wasn't ever enough left over to buy a bus or train ticket so his wife and children could join him. She had missed him so much that finally she packed all their clothes in a couple of old suitcases, gathered up the children and had slipped aboard a freight train headed in the direction where her husband was working. It was a stupid thing to do and she realized it now. It had been four days since they left; and of course, during this time the car had been shifted from one train to another, so that by now she was lost, and exhausted, afraid and hungry. Out of sheer luck this train she and her children were on was actually headed toward the town she had mentioned and would arrive there early the next morning. Once the woman had found this out she was determined to stay in the car until it arrived. This had put the railroad official in the awkward position of either doing his duty and throwing her and the children off, or turning his back, and letting them go on. However, just letting them go wouldn't be enough because she was weak from hunger and so were her children. Also, as he had explained to Maud, it was just a miracle that worse things hadn't happened to this defenseless woman, alone in a boxcar, considering that some of the men riding the trains were not very civilized.

Knowing Maud, I could understand why the bull had finally brought the whole problem and dumped it into her hands. Maud was ready to go immediately with food for the mother and kids, even over the protests of the railroad bull. He had a hard time stopping her but was finally able to convince her that he would lose his job and the woman would be kicked off if she did that, because they would be discovered. This was where I came in since I was leaving town anyway they decided that I could take a flour sack filled with bottles of milk and food to her, and would be able to jump aboard without being seen. The railroad bull would point out the car they were in, and then I could deliver the food. Maud had also become quite insistent, that not only was I to deliver the food, but I was to stay with the woman and her children, look out for them and deliver them to their husband and father. She went on to say that I was a good boy and that she knew she could depend on me to get this job done. And I guess if Maud thought I could do it, then I thought I could do it too. The railroad bull and I went down to the tracks and he pointed out the car they were in. Then he gripped my arm till it hurt, while he told me to jump into the car, slide the door shut, leaving a six inch gap, wedge it from the inside, and then guard the woman and children. I was not to leave the car or open the door until we got into the town. Then he went on to say that he would get word to the yard bull where we were going, and that he would help get us out of the yards. After giving me his night stick and telling me to use it if necessary, he left.

Everything went as planned. I climbed into the car, gave the sack to the woman and was actually embarrassed as she thanked me over and over again, as she fed herself and the children. I was not sure how all of this happened; but I did know that I felt very proud that someone could de-pend on me for protection. As I fixed the car door there was no question in my mind that I would fight and possibly even kill someone if they tried to harm them. Then I stood there looking out of the crack in the door as we left the little town behind. I thought of Maud and how basically good she was and I thought of Jack and Mary. When I thought of Jack and of his stories about all his girls, especially Mary, I finally concluded that he was one of the world's greatest liars.

One of the children in the car was a little girl, who seemed to be about three years old. Her hair was so matted and full of dirt that there was no way of knowing its natural color. She was wearing a long old-style dress that came almost to her ankles. The only clean place on her seemed to be a part of her face, where tears had washed little gullies through the accumulated dirt. Her eyes were like two bright blue lakes, set on the side of a brown mountain; while her tear streaked cheeks looked like dried up stream beds. I was sitting against the wall on the opposite side of the car from the partially open door. The train had picked up speed so that the old familiar clickity clack of the wheels was having its usual soothing effect on me The little girl walked over to me and with feet firmly planted against the sway of the car stood solemnly staring into my face. In one tightly closed, grimy fist, she was clutching a piece of bread from her dinner. With me sitting and her standing our eyes were almost on the same level. I got the most disconcerted feeling because she was staring directly at me, without the slightest change of expression or without even blinking.

I began to shift restlessly, had dropped my eyes and was almost ready to get up to escape that penetrating look, when suddenly she held out her hand with the piece of bread in it. It was such a quick, involuntary gesture, that I had no choice but to take it. She plopped herself down beside me and arranged her dirty dress, like the grandest lady of the land; and again gave me such a direct look that I had no choice but to eat every bit of that bread down to the last crumb.

Satisfied, she snuggled against my side laid her head on my chest, gave one tremulous sigh of complete faith and went soundly to sleep. I glanced quickly at her mother, but she surprised me; as she didn't act like she was too worried about what was taking place. In fact with her small smile and slight nod, it became apparent that they all felt like they were in good hands and could all lay down to rest. The sleeping children and their mother had all placed their safety in my hands and having done it with such obvious confidence that it was a new and strange experience for me.

The little girl was warm against my side with one hand clinging tightly to my shirt, even as she slept. Her baby smell even though it was mingled with dirt and boxcar smells, and absolute helplessness created such a strong fierce protective urge in me that I was overwhelmed with emotion.

I had become the protective male and I sat alertly, surveying my charges, as the train rushed on its way.

Night came and went with nothing more eventful happening than one or another of the children awakening at different times. They would whimper with fear of the darkness and the strange sounds; and then I would hear their mother crooning softly and reassuringly to them. Soon all would be quiet again. My personal charge seemed to sleep the soundest of all. I sat for so long without moving that my body began to ache all over and my arm against which she was leaning seemed completely paralyzed. At one time during the night I simply had to lay her on the floor so that I could stand up and stretch. She immediately started to whimper so I quickly sat back down. I was sure that when morning came my arm would just fall off at the shoulder as it was now numb and without feeling but I didn't care.

All of the boxcars have a number painted on their sides. These numbers were large and easily read, and were there for use by switchmen and other railroad men who were engaged in switching or routing cars to their proper destination. The number on our car had been given to the railroad bull in the town into which we were now pulling. The train had no sooner stopped than a man was at the door ordering us to hurry up and get out. He was a huge bear of a man with a three or four day's growth of black whiskers. His low sloping forehead disappeared abruptly under the brim of his hat. His small agate eyes glistened from under bushy eyebrows and his whole appearance was like that of pictures I had seen of apes in the depths of an African jungle.

Quickly I slid the door open and handed him the children. My little girl was last, and I noticed that he handled her longer than was necessary before finally putting her on the ground. I then hopped down and prepared to help the children's mother get out of the car. There was just no way that a woman with a dress on, could climb out of a boxcar, without showing some leg and maybe even her underwear. The mother, with her nervousness and inexperience, stood over our heads and extended one foot as though she could just step out onto the ground. In doing this of course, she was completely exposed. She had a fine body with long shapely legs and thighs and was wearing only a thin pair of panties. The narrow strip of cloth between her legs was seductively imbedded, leaving open to our view the soft rounded sides with their covering of black curly pubic hair. She was a completely desirable female in this moment, more so than if she had been completely naked.

I heard an sharp involuntary intake of breath from the railroad bull, when she finally sat down so that we could help her out. His hands were trembling slightly and as I looked into his eyes, they had become small red pinpoints of light. Even I had felt a primitive male desire and I knew without question, that had this man found her alone, he would have satisfied his basic biological need. He would have stripped away that flimsy barrier of cloth as easily as he would have laid aside a thousand years of civilization, then he would have satisfied himself using her body with no more qualms of conscience than he would have had in eating food when he was hungry.

Even now he was only controlling himself with effort. Both the mother and I were fearful. She, being female, had immediately sensed her danger and seemed to shrink back as though expecting a blow. I was scared too because I knew I would be no match for this man if he lost his thin thread of control. Should this have happened I would have been no more threat to him than any other young male trying to challenge the superior rights of the fittest. He could have broken my back and brushed me aside as easily as he would have swatted an irritating fly. We didn't need his curt, "Beat it," to quickly gather up the children and leave.

From a safe distance away I looked back to find him still watching us, or to be more exact, watching the woman. I lagged a few steps behind in helping the children and as I glanced at her buttocks moving under her thin dress I'll be damned if they didn't seem to be twitching from side to side much more than was necessary for her to walk. I couldn't believe any woman would be physically attracted to a man like that; yet her narrow escape from being forcibly taken must have stirred some primitive, deeply buried response in her body also. In fairness I doubt if she was even aware of her actions.

As I openly watched her now with pleasure, I could see again the picture she presented in trying to step out of the boxcar; and it made me wonder. There was no question that this woman was basically fine and decent. Because of her basic decency, she had risked her very life and that of her children, to be with a man who could satisfy her physical needs in a legal manner. No other animal except humans seem to go to this much trouble. As I continued to watch her and think about our long night together in that boxcar, I questioned which of us was the more sensible; the woman with the terrible risks she had taken; I with my young idealism; or the railroad bull whose simple instincts could have solved the problem in a matter of minutes.

I'm still not sure who was right, yet I did decide that the next time the opportunity presented itself, I would keep an open mind on the subject.

The mother, the three children and I made a strange procession as we walked down the sidewalk. People stared at us with amusement and it was easy to see why. The mother was about as bedraggled as any person could be and so were the children. You could imagine how they must have looked, after almost a week in a boxcar, without a bath or even a way to wash their faces. Added to this odd picture, was me carrying a baby on one arm and lugging a suitcase in my other hand. What questions must have been going through their minds. They were probably speculating as to whether or not I was the father of that mob; while reason told them that I looked too young; but on the other hand I looked too old to be another one of her children. Their dilemma was amusing to me, but also somewhat embarrassing, so it was a relief when we finally turned into the lobby of a hotel and escaped the many eyes.

Even the hotel clerk's face registered some dismay when he saw this strange looking group approach the desk. I was proud of the mother, because with dignity and confidence, she made arrangements for a room. Now that she was safe and back in an acceptable element she spoke in a no nonsense voice that demanded respect in spite of her appearance. I felt that my job was finished; and that Maud would be pleased and proud of me. At the same time it was a big relief not to have this responsibility any longer. As I stood there, impatient to leave, the mother came over to me. Taking both my hands in hers she stood quietly looking into my face. The pressure of her fingers on mine, and the expression on her face told me her thanks in a way that a thousand profuse words could never have done.

The little girl was tugging on my pant leg so I knelt down and received a wet and sloppy kiss on my cheek. This, then, was the way we parted; and it was good to be outside on the sidewalk again, free of any worries except taking care of myself. After that experience it seemed like that would be a cinch.

What a grand and glorious world I thought it was. This was a big city and I was impressed by the tall buildings and amazed at the crowds of people hurrying in all directions. Each of them moved along quickly, faces set with determination and dedication, to some unknown destination. How fortunate I felt to be free and just stand and watch. I was even glad I had no family ties, no memories of love or home that could cause me regrets in this moment. I was young and healthy, it was springtime and I was filled with joy at my own self sufficiency.

There were no pressures facing me except getting something to eat and finding a place to sleep. Even if I had not had almost three dollars in my pocket I knew that I could find food; because while working at Maud's Cafe, I had heard every possible story and had learned the tone of voice and facial expressions to go with it. These were sound lessons of survival that had to be learned if a man were to adapt himself to a particular circumstance. It was true with creatures of the forest and was just as true in this jungle of the day. I had learned my lessons well and felt I would never find myself going hungry. With my rolled up blankets, the whole world was my bed. I could sleep in the middle, at the foot or on either side. The choice was mine.

My step was light and carefree as I set out to see more of these new and wonderful sights. I walked along, sometimes looking upward, with awe at the height of buildings; and I was sure that I was a true picture of a simple country boy coming to the big city for the first time. Even the traffic lights fascinated me and I stood on the corner watching large groups of people take turns at movement. They were all striding purposely along, then suddenly stop completely and stand almost immovable at the curb. Every eye was concentrated on a little square box mounted on a post across the street. This little box was a complete dictator and regardless of the impatience or importance of a person, it never changed its timing or showed any favoritism.

Its baleful red eye held them all pinned to the spot until it suddenly said, "WALK!" and by damn, then and only then, did people walk. Some stepped right out with confidence, while others gave an involuntary start before getting underway. It appeared that they were so regimented by signals, whistles, and bells that it took a second for their mind to relay the message to their feet that it was all right to move. The whole operation was performed with a background of sound beyond comprehension. Brakes squealing, horns blowing, huge trucks bellowing defiance at each other while grinding their gears with rage, as they raced one another to the next intersection, only to be stopped again. And poor insignificant man, who had created this monster in the first place, now danced to its tune performing their steps in unison, first on one curb, then on the other. I became one of them also and had no intention of questioning the authority of that inanimate, but indomitable, blood-shot eye on the post.

It didn't seem possible, but after walking for several blocks through noise and confusion, there before my eyes were trees and green grass. It was a park set right in the middle of this huge city. I wandered around breathing deeply of the clean fresh air. There was also a small lake; and on its surface, ducks and geese swam around just as nonchalantly as any duck had back on the pond at the Jackson's. Even the people were a surprise. Some were just sitting quietly in the sun, while the ones who were walking around moved at a leisurely pace, stopping to watch a child play or to chat with some acquaintance.

What a contrast it was! I could still hear the roar of the frantic city in the background; but in the park the noise was muffled and had to compete with the joyous sounds of children playing, and the songs of birds. The birds were hard to hear but they were there if you listened intently. I had to grudgingly revise some of my first thoughts about the men responsible for the city and give them credit for creating this island of paradise in the very midst of what appeared to be disorganized chaos. This profound observation on my part was soon to be shot to hell. The green grass was soft and the shade provided by one of the many leafy trees was so inviting, that I stretched out on the ground under one of them to take a nap. Using my bedroll for a pillow, and with the clear conscience of youth, I quickly fell asleep.

I didn't know if I were dreaming or what fantasies I may have been indulging in while asleep, but I was sure that none of them were in accord with the painful stinging blow I was suddenly receiving on the bottom of my feet. It was such a shocking and abrupt awakening from a sound sleep that when I opened my eyes, all I could see was blue. It was a second or two before I realized that the sky hadn't really changed color, but that this blue was the blue of a uniform being worn by a very threatening policeman. I was to find out that what I had thought to be confusion and turmoil in the city was actually a well run and highly efficient system; and the responsibility for keeping it that way was in the hands of several hundred well trained men, one of whom was standing over me right at this moment.

I was also to learn that there were different classes of society. This park was provided and maintained for use by respectable and. productive members of the city; and by no means was it meant to be used by riffraff, bums, or vagrants who might think it would be a good place for a nap. I gathered from the officer's tone of voice that I fell into the latter category and maybe even into all three. In any case there was no question in my mind that I was being hustled along beside him to the nearest call box. In a matter of minutes a patrol wagon arrived and I couldn't help but compare the similarity of my situation to the times we used to load cattle for the market. There too, a truck arrived, a back door opened and the animals were herded inside. Here, when the police van arrived I was shoved into the van, which was full with other men, and as the door closed behind me, I knew just how those cows must have felt.

When we arrived at the police station the van door was opened and we were prodded rapidly along a narrow chute like hallway that opened up into a large room. This was all very bewildering and strange to me, and I felt a sense of panic, knowing that I was penned up. I found that this large room was called the tank, and all in-coming men were herded into it. Those who were drunk, were just left there until they sobered up. For many of the drunks and habitual winos, this was a familiar routine, and they were already making themselves comfortable by laying on the floor or sitting against the wall.

The other men watched me with amusement because I looked scared, and it was obvious that this was my first time. Their easy acceptance of what had happened to them had its effect on me, and I began to relax a little bit. However, along with the relaxation, I began to feel the beginning of resentment and rebellion. This was supposed to be a free country, yet here I was, pushed, shoved and finally locked up, just for sleeping on the grass. The more I thought about it the more outraged I became; so that when a guard motioned for me to follow him, I did so with ill concealed contempt and obvious anger.

He took me before a woman, who was the City Judge. From her appearance and age, she had probably sat there for thirty years, during which time she had undoubtedly tried to be fair and impartial in her judgment of all the varied crimes people had committed, and then paraded before her. I was convinced too, that when she looked at my young face she would know immediately that I was no criminal! So, when she asked me if I was guilty or not guilty to a charge of vagrancy, I resented this question and was very emphatic in saying, "Hell No! I am not guilty", and went into a childish tirade about my free country, justice and "who in hell had the right to do this to me anyway?" and so on.

It all sounded so good and enlightening to me that it was some time before I finally ran down. During all of this she just sat there looking kind of bored and indifferent. When I finally realized no one was paying the least bit of attention to me, I shut up. I should have shut up much sooner because this wise old woman then said, "Young man, your crime of sleeping on the grass would have gotten you nothing more than a warning, and a request to obey the law in the future. Now however, since you have spent ten minutes instructing everyone within hearing distance about justice you leave me with no choice but to impose the just penalty for vagrancy. I sentence you to thirty days or thirty dollars"!

As I have said the people in this city were organized; so well organized in fact that in the space of a few hours I was changed from a lighthearted, free as a bird, cocky, young man, to a little wiser locked up young man, sitting on a hard bunk in a jail cell. I was a little hurt that no one had appreciated my eloquence in court. I still felt that it had been a pretty good speech. Yet I had a sneaking suspicion that maybe the old judge had heard it before. She hadn't seemed impressed.

The cell was about ten feet square. The front of the cell which faced the hall had steel bars set about four inches apart which ran from floor to ceiling. A door also made of bars was set in the center. It was hinged on one side and had a large square built-in lock on the other. The key hole in this lock looked just like any ordinary house lock; but it was much bigger. The key itself was almost six inches long. The sides of the cell were concrete and provided a common wall between the adjoining cells. On each of these side walls hung two bunks. They were nothing more than two planks held together by three strips of iron, two bolted to ends and one in the center. From each of these end strips a small chain ran up to the concrete wall where it was also fastened securely.

With this construction the planks hung from the wall, supported by the chains, with all the bolts and nuts flattened in such a manner that no one could possibly take them apart, to gain a weapon. Each bunk had a thin cotton pad which certainly shouldn't be called a mattress. It was almost as hard as the planks were without it. My bunk was the top left hand one and as I stretched out on the hard unyielding pad, I thought of the feather bed I had slept in at the Jackson's. Now that was a mattress!

Along the back wall was a wash basin with one single faucet that ran only cold water. Next to the wash basin was a toilet. This toilet was different from any I had ever seen. It was made completely from metal, even the seat. This seat was always cold on your bare bottom when you sat down but the strangest and most unusual feature of this toilet, though was that when you sat on the seat, your weight opened a water valve, so that all during your stay there, the action was accompanied by the noisy, rushing sounds of water.

I put off using it just as long as possible, not only because of the noise but also because of the complete lack of privacy. This was only in my own mind for finally I could wait no longer and found no one paid the slightest attention to me. I found this toilet to be a very efficient method for not only washing the bowl clean, but also the person. Above the basin and toilet was a small square barred window. It provided some ventilation and by peering upward at an angle, I could see just a patch of blue sky. I had learned to accept things as they came, but this was a very depressing place to be. I had been picked up about noon before I'd had a chance to rustle some food, so by now I was getting very hungry. I assumed that someone would feed us but I wasn't even too sure about that. My imagination could very easily dwell on the possibility of starving to death. And as hungry as I am right now it wouldn't take very long.

But I was happy and relieved to see that we would be fed. First each prisoner was handed a tin bowl and one tablespoon; then down the hall came a four wheeled cart with a huge kettle of soup sitting on it. The cart was pushed by one guard, and as he stopped in front of each cell, another guard took the tin bowl you are holding out between the bars and ladled it full of soup. At the same time everyone got a slice of bread. In watching the men in the cell across the hall from me I was reminded of a bunch of monkeys at the zoo. They too were locked up, and would extend their arms through the bars as far as possible. I used to think they were reaching for the occasional peanut thrown their way, but in watching the men in this jail, and with how I was feeling I wondered if they were trying to get as much of their body free as the bars would allow.

I also remembered the sounds that were made by locked up animals when their feeding time came. Some would roar, others whimpered, or gave excited barks of impatience. It seemed no different here, as the cart moved along. Some of those who had already gotten their food were cursing the food in loud obscenities, while others were banging their tin bowls against the bars, and cursing equally as loud trying to get the guards to hurry. My turn finally came and I was so grateful for that tepid, watery bowl of soup, and slice of stale bread, that I even thanked the guard. He looked at me like I was some kind of an idiot; which, of course I was. These men in jail could have cared less what the food was or even how it tasted. Their cursing was the only way they could retain some bit of dignity and independence while they were locked up. I realized too that there was a tremendous difference between the noises the animals made and the ones these caged men made. The animals cried from physical hunger, while these men were reacting from a sense of despair at being forcibly separated from the human race.

There was soup left over and this was given to a few of the prisoners who hadn't been quite so outspoken in their opinions about the guards' ancestry and origin. Even though the guards had heard it all many times and didn't seem to pay much attention to these personal attacks, when it was possible to hand out seconds they became very selective. I was one of those chosen to receive this extra portion and only the fact that I was young and could eat anything made this second bowl of now cold, almost tasteless soup have any real meaning. Shortly after all of us had been fed, the naked bulb hanging high on the ceiling of each cell was turned off; and the jail, was plunged into darkness. I laid stretched out on my top bunk, with my hands under my head, and thought about the last few days. I was surprised when I thought about all that had taken place and how quickly things had changed. I thought of Maud and wished I were there in her big bed with my face laying close to her full mature breasts. We would have satisfied one of my first needs by now and would be laying quietly fulfilling another equally great need. She was the mother; and I was the child at her breast. In my present state of loneliness I missed her very much.

I also thought about the woman and her children, and the many hours we had spent together riding the boxcar. I pictured what a nice looking family they must have made when cleaned up, especially the little girl with her hair combed and her face scrubbed, wearing a clean dress. I shared in the joy the father must have felt when he saw his family after such a long time. And even though my eyes were averted still I was there when they got into bed and I silently urged them on to greater and more frenzied efforts as they attempted to make up for lost time.

Finally I thought of me, and this was with the greatest wonderment of all, because I began to feel that I was moving through life, even though it seemed aimless and without purpose, toward some prearranged destiny. I realized that I might just as well accept each day with calmness until I reached that destiny. This conclusion right or wrong had a quieting effect on my mind and I went soundly to sleep.

Morning came or I supposed it was morning. There was no way of knowing, except that suddenly the lights came on; and one of the guards walked the full length of the hall, down one side and back up the other. In one hand he had one of the tin bowls which he dragged along the bars much like a child drags a stick along a picket fence. In the narrow confines of the jail, this racket was enough to awaken a dead person. Again, he was thoroughly cursed; and I was amazed at the vehemence and feeling that was put into this by some of the men. Their tone of voice and select choice of words showed an absolute hatred for the guard and indirectly, for the system he represented.

I couldn't quite understand this, because in most cases they were here because of actions or crimes they had committed; and it seemed to me that they should realize that their present plight was the direct result of these actions and that they had to share at least some of the responsibility. Not all of it by any means, because even I had already seen so much hunger and despair in so many faces that I could partly understand their feelings. I guess the thing that bothered me was their violent and extreme way of fighting back. I was more inclined to relax and accept things as they came.

In any case it was all wasted effort on their part; because the expression-less guard completed his noisy task of getting everyone up with complete indifference. My belief in passive acceptance was probably good; but unfortunately it lasted only until the door opened at the end of the hall; and what looked like the same huge kettle that our soup was in was wheeled in. Steam was rising from it in great clouds, and my stomach immediately began to churn with anticipation. I was too far down the hall to see what it was and didn't really care. It was obviously hot and I was so hungry that I knew I could just dive into that kettle, swim around and eat my fill.

I didn't realize until later but this feeding wasn't accompanied by the usual ribald comments. There were just the sounds of cell doors opening and of what I thought were the sounds of tin bowls being filled with food. I was crowded up against the front of my cell, waiting with eagerness for it to come into view. I smelled it before I could even see it; and it had a pungent smell so strong that it almost hurt my eyes. The thought did pass through my mind, that I hoped it tasted better than it smelled. Finally it was here; and I received such a shock that I had to hang onto the bars for a moment in complete disbelief. What I had thought to be hot steaming food, probably mush, turned out to be a hot steaming kettle of water. The unsavory smell came from bars of yellow lye soap floating around in it. What I had thought to be the sound of bowls being filled was actually the sound of tin buckets being filled with water and set in front of each cell. With each bucket, instead of a piece of bread, there was a mop. Now I understood the strange quietness in the jail. The men were embarrassed in suffering this final blow to their dignity and self respect by being made to sweep and mop the floor.

It was more than I was able to accept, and in my disappointment and anger at being fooled into thinking it was food, I made up my mind that I wouldn't mop their floor, even if they killed me. So when the guard opened the cell door to hand me the mop, I just stood there glaring and refused to take it. I was ready to curse and scream my anger and even fight if needed to, but I was met with that same indifference, as the guard handed the mop to one of the other men and moved on. I felt that I had won a victory of some kind, yet, I was a little uneasy because as I looked at the other men, some of whom had cursed the loudest in rebellion, I wasn't sure what my victory was. They may not have been mopping the damn floor gracefully, but they were mopping it. I found out why when it finally came time to have breakfast.

The same routine was followed as the night before, with one notable exception. When I held out my hand for my bowl it was as casually ignored, as I had ignored the mop. I thought for a moment it was just an oversight and that the guard had not seen my hand. I was just ready to open my mouth and bring it to his attention, when the cold realization hit me that I wasn't going to be fed. Then I was glad that I hadn't said anything, because my pride was involved, so I just silently thought, "Well, piss on you, you, son of a bitch, take your mush and shove it up your ass!" These sentiments were great and I managed to substitute them in the place of food all morning. At noon I didn't even lower my pride enough to get down off my bunk and act like I was hungry. It's a good thing the guard didn't ask me if I wanted lunch because, BOY, would I have told him off! I spent a good hour after everyone else had eaten just lying there thinking of all the things I could have told him and where he could go. Sometime late in the afternoon my violent feelings of hate and anger began to dissolve and were replaced with a new emotion. The change was a gradual thing, but soon I began to be filled with an overwhelming sense of self pity. Now I lay there, a true martyr, ready and willing to die a slow and painful death from starvation, just to get even. While they were feeding everyone else their supper meal, I lay on my bunk with my face toward the wall. I wanted to be sure the guard got one last look at this pitiful sight while I was still alive, so that he could remember it the rest of his life. Because, I thought the next time he sees my face it will be dead and pinched from hunger and cold. I was even thinking, that I could be noble enough to spare him this sight, if he wanted to ask me to eat. But again he hardly looked at me, so I am resolved to die.

One of the other men in my cell was selected for seconds at supper so instead of eating it, he brought it over to me. At first, with all my resolve I almost refused, but then I thought that if I were going to die anyway, this little bit wouldn't be enough to make any difference. So I practically inhaled it! At the same time, as I looked into his kindly face I was filled with a great love for him; and I was glad that someone cared enough to give me one last kindness before I passed on. The next time I saw his kindly face was sometime during the night when I felt his hands on my body.

There was just enough light filtering into the cell from the barred window for me to see that it was the same man. When I first woke up and realized what was going on, I almost smashed my fist into his face. Then I guess I finally just gave up. I laid back and allowed the not too unpleasant sensation of feeling him play with my penis. When he finally placed it in his mouth, and in the last seconds of thrusting climax, each thrust was accompanied with a silent, "Fuck you, old man; fuck you guard, fuck you life!" And with the final thrust of release came, "Fuck this idea of starving to death!" With this much needed relief from emotional and physical tension, I fell back, again going soundly to sleep.

Morning came again in exactly the same manner as before. First the lights flashed on, then came the nerve shattering sounds of the tin bowl being dragged along the bars. I awoke with some new thoughts and with a changed outlook on my situation. First, I realized that the systematic routine of running this jail would defeat any independent displays of rebellion such as I had had yesterday. The management of this hotel, with its captive guests, was in absolute control. The very indifference to any ranting and raving by their guests was their greatest weapon. My own experience had proved this beyond any doubt. With them having the keys to freedom and either giving food or withholding it, put them in a position of supreme control. I would have been stupid not to realize this and only hurt myself by not seeing it sooner. This time, when the guard opened our cell door and handed me the mop, I took it without hesitation and kept my face as expressionless as his own. When I did this a strange thing happened. He actually looked at me for the first time, like I was another human being, and smiled. I had to smile back because I knew what he was thinking. That son of a bitch had known how it would turn out all the time.

I did my share of mopping, doing it quickly and efficiently and later as I held my bowl through the bars, it was filled with food just as quickly and efficiently. I had learned another very basic and important lesson about life from this experience. Do not try to change something when it is obvious that there is no way to do it.

Life was like a river and as long as I was in it, I should learn to swim better. A good swimmer never wears himself out by continually swimming upstream against the current; and will occasionally just drift. This looked like a time for drifting. One thing about being in jail was that there was plenty of time for thinking. This was a doubtful benefit to be sure, but nevertheless time dragged so slowly, that sooner or later you were bound to think about something, just because there was absolutely nothing else to do.

The man in the cell with me gave me much food for thought. This was the second person who, like Mr. Jackson, apparently suffered from the same perversion. I simply could not understand this desire for sexual gratification with another man. To me, the act seemed like the most sickening and disgusting thing a person could possibly do. I tried to examine all parts of this question, setting all moral aspects aside, and putting it on an all-compelling, purely sexual need, and it still ended up as something I would never do. The baffling thing was not to be able to see any visible signs in their looks or behavior that would identify them. Certainly Mr. Jackson was basically a good and religious man desperately trying to live a decent life.

Even my cell mate appears to be reasonably intelligent. In fact, from the look of his clothes, he must have been moderately successful in a job or a business of his own. Yet, whatever the mysterious reasons for his homosexuality, it was so great that he was known and had been picked up, just for loitering around the men's restroom at a bus terminal. But the most enlightening thing to me was the easy acceptance of his sexual orientation by the other men in jail. My first reaction to him had been one of contempt and rejection; the same contempt I had felt for Mr. Jackson. Now I was surprised to find what I came to accept as the first really true brotherhood of man. I had never felt this as strongly as now, even while sitting in church surrounded by pious members who were programmed into thinking they had all the answers to salvation. Every man in this jail knew why this man was here and yet not one of them ridiculed him or degraded him. They accepted his faults easily, without making judgments, simply because each of them must know that they, too, were far from perfect.

Many of the men in this jail were habitual offenders against the man-made rules of society, yet they displayed a high degree of compassion and tolerance toward the faults of others. Jesus said, "if there be one among you without sin let him cast the first stone."

As I looked around me at this odd mixture of humans and how they acted toward one another, His teaching seemed to take on real meaning for me for the first time.

It was all very confusing and now I was completely mixed up about how I should feel toward this man. Last night I had been vulnerable, and had submitted to his demands. I had been lonely and so lost that almost any gesture made by another person would have been accepted. My state of mind was so depressed that being needed for any reason had been welcome.

But this morning I was ashamed. I thought that everyone would be pointing a mental finger at me, knowing what I had allowed to happen. When it came time to get up, I laid there just as long as possible, not wanting to face the humiliation. I felt that they must know, especially the other two men in the cell, but no one with even the slightest gesture or word, made any reference to what had taken place; and the day started with the same usual routine.

But, I had to resolve this thing in my mind. The other men and their complete indifference forced me to put the experience in a completely new perspective. I had reacted as any person would, who was raised under the influence of society's stereotyped beliefs. The men in this jail were another part of society, also with beliefs and a culture, except that this one seemed to have much deeper insight and ability to accept human frailties without pretense and hypocrisy. So I will face the honest fact, and admit I enjoyed the sexual climax of last night. Sex is a fiercely demanding hunger in my body, an urge that is never satisfied, and hadn't been even with Maud. One time with her, some nights, was like giving a man a sip of water when he is dying of thirst. I knew without question that had she allowed me to, I could have kept her awake all night, satisfying this unquenchable hunger.

It seems to me that every young, healthy male is the same way and usually has limited outlets. I think that most young girls are the same way too, but unfortunately, like Mary, are frustrated by society's imposed restrictions on females. Often, the result of these restrictions is that when they finally marry, they cannot accept sex and many of them turn into nagging neurotics, alcoholics, and finally inevitably divorced. If a marriage goes on the rocks, the rocks could very well be under the mattress.

Mother nature gave me this erection and left me with no physical doubts, at least, as to what to do with it. And since her overall scheme of things seems to have been better planned than what man has been able to come up with, I guess I'll go along with her wisdom. So my poor mixed up friend, since I'm locked up in this cell, you will become a very poor substitute indeed. Even so, it is more gratifying than masturbation and if I refrain from that you are most certainly better than the nocturnal wet dream that is sure to follow. So now the issue has become clear; and tonight I will lay on my side in my top bunk facing outward. I will cooperate in every way to make this experience as fulfilling to him as his strange need requires. I'll not attempt to justify either his reasons or mine, because I know I am not wise enough to do so. Each of us will have a need relieved, he much more so than I. He was willing to share his food with me when I was hungry; and maybe that too is part of the final answer.

In any case this particular problem was solved the next day when this man was released. There were no fond farewells or good byes said by anyone. As he left the cell his eyes met mine for a moment, and he raised

his fingers to his forehead, giving me a wry salute. His face was without
expression, and he didn't say a word, yet the gesture was one I could return
with equal recognition. A short time later I was free also. He evidently did
have money, because he had paid the remainder of my fine on his way out
of the jail.

Quickly I collected my bedroll and hurried outside. I felt I should thank
him, but he was gone. I guess it was for the best, because many of my
questions and much of my hurt from Mr. Jackson had left me. And had I
tried to thank him for these things he could never have understood. So
which causes the greater harm: Spending the rest of my life hating Mr.
Jackson; or my now having gained some measure of understanding and
tolerance because of this supposedly unspeakable dirty experience. I knew
that now I could possibly return to the only home I have ever had for a
visit.

I had thought it would be fun to stay in this city for awhile, find a job, a
place to live, and see more of the sights; but this particular city has dealt
with me roughly and it was only because of an odd circumstance that I was
free. Also, my stay in jail, though very educational had not been pleasant,
and I felt a dirtiness of mind and spirit that only the quiet stillness of the
country-side could cleanse. The physical act that I had allowed to happen
to me was nothing compared to the state of mind that can develop from
being closely confined with grown men. These were grown men who were
outcasts from society, many of whom saw nothing good in life worth
striving for, had become human parasites, without hope. Their only purpose was to survive without effort, and they did this by stealing, begging or
any other means just as long as they escaped all responsibility.

I was young and couldn't accept their total rejection of what I guess must
be called hope or faith. I still wanted to hope and retain some faith that
people would give to each other just for the satisfaction of giving. Maud
had done so a hundred times, giving food to hungry strangers for no other
reason than compassion.

I needed to see some trees and grass that were just there, and know that if I wanted to lay in the shade of a tree for a few minutes while passing by, no one would really care. Tonight I will lay on my blanket and see a million stars instead of just one that shines through a small barred window.

THE ORPHAN

CHAPTER 4
SUFFICIENCY WITHIN MYSELF

I hurried, almost with fear, from what had happened to me and already the fields were in sight. They were as vast as the sky; and I soon selected a place to stop. I won't take up much room out here and in the morning when the sun rose to warm me, then I believed I would feel clean and free again.

The place was ideal. There was a small stream running through a culvert under the highway. This little stream was a long way from home, just as I was, and yet it had found its way all by itself, far from the blue haze of mountains in the distance. It just traveled along, sounding happy, sometimes running fast, and other times resting quietly in little pools. And just like me, occasionally it went around in circles getting nowhere.

By one of these pools was a grassy bank, shaded by a huge tree, many years old. It was so large that its shade not only covered the bank but extended across a quiet pond causing the water to have a cool inviting look. This was the place; and the first thing I did was strip completely, then jumped joyously into the water. How good it felt and I even washed all my clothes hanging them on bushes to dry, while I continued to play in the pool. All of a sudden I got the feeling I was not alone, that someone or something was watching me. When I stopped playing to look around there were two young men standing on the bank. My position was not the best since I was naked and in water up to my waist, and they were on the bank. Also there was the fact that there were two of them. We silently surveyed each other and I realized that they were as surprised to see me as I was to see them. Finally one of them asked, "How's the water?" "It's fine," I replied. "Come on in." "Don't you have a suit on?" "Hell no!, there's not a soul within ten miles of here, besides if they don't know what it looks like by now it's time they did." With this they both laughed and quickly stripped off their clothes. One of them got back about fifteen feet, then ran and with a tremendous leap, landed in the water. In minutes we were all three splashing each other and having a great time. Finally, we flopped on the cool grass to rest and dry off. It had been fun. I had enjoyed the spontaneous horse-play with someone my own age. One of the boys was tall and lanky, built about the same as I, while the other was a good six inches shorter, but with a compact stocky body.

He had been the one jumping into the water and after we had rested for awhile he said, "My name is Paul Saxton and this is Dick Bessington. What are you doing all alone out here in the middle of nowhere?" "Just call me Slim, and I'm not doing a damn thing. I'm just passing through the country and this looked like a good place to spend the night."

"Well it sure is that" Dick commented, "I wouldn't mind staying here myself. Why don't you?" It was hard for me to keep the hope out of my voice, because I did want their company. "It's a nice spot and there is plenty of room." "You're sure you don't care?", asked Dick. "Hell no. Let's get dressed. Where did you stash your bedrolls? Out by the highway? Go get them and I'll build a fire. I've got two cans of beans we can eat." I said all this in practically one breath and was almost like a puppy wriggling with eagerness to please. Paul said, "We don't have a bedroll but we've got some blankets in the car." "Car! You mean you guys have a car. Where is it? What kind is it? Jesus Christ, let's go see it." I couldn't believe that anybody actually had a car. Lots of people drove cars but to really have a car of your own was something you just didn't even dream about because it seemed so impossible.

But they did have a car. It was an old '28 Chrysler four-door sedan sitting right beside the highway. I walked around it with awe admiring the long hood and the big, old square body. It was simply beautiful. The back seat was piled full of their stuff, blankets, a couple of camp stools and even pots and pans to cook with. I was very impressed and felt they were high society. "Boy", I said, "what a luxurious way to travel." Dick had been looking around and now he said, "Say, I think we can drive right over to our camping spot. What do you think, Slim?" I became all business and answered this serious question with an equally thoughtful reply, "Yeah, I think you can. Take it slow. I'll walk ahead and watch for holes and rocks." The spot I had picked was only about a quarter mile from the highway and the trip was made without any trouble. They unloaded all their stuff and in a few minutes we had a camp set up. I found some rocks to put around our fire, dumped my two cans of beans in one of their pots and set it on one of the rocks to get warm. They even had some spuds to slice and fry and before long we had a meal fit for kings. After eating we all laid back, just silently staring at the flames. I don't know about their feelings, but for me, I was fully content and felt happier than I had ever felt before in my life. I had two friends, even if only for a little while, and on top of that they had a car.

They must have been filled with their own thoughts as no one was saying much, except for a passing observation like, "Gee, it's quiet," or "Don't the stars look close tonight?" Paul said, "Did you ever wonder about the stars? I wonder if anyone lives on any of them. Maybe there are people just like us out there." Then we all lay silently wondering about this too, each of us with our own separate imagination.

I'd had a long day and was tired from walking so far, and was about to go to sleep. I didn't want to because I wanted so much to share their companionship around the glowing coals of our fire. But even they were beginning to get drowsy, so we all fixed our beds and crawled in. I lay there thinking, while listening to a small breeze sigh through the leaves of the big tree, about how great it would be if I could travel with them. The little stream was gurgling softly in the darkness. Dick must have been listening to its sound too, because the last thing I heard was a sleepy, "I'll bet there's some fish in that creek."

I must have really been tired because I didn't wake up all night and probably wouldn't have awakened when I did, except that suddenly I sat straight up; hearing somebody yelling, "I got one, I got one!" It was broad daylight and Paul was sitting up also with the same startled look on his face.

"What the hells going on?", he asked. "I'll be darned if I know. Where's Dick?" but, even as I asked I could see Dick. He must have had fish on his mind all night and as soon as it was light enough to see, he had cut a willow, tied on some line and a hook and was fishing. Not only was he fishing but a second yell let us know he was catching some.

"Well, for Pete's sake," I said, "let's go before he catches all of them." Paul was full of instant excitement, as he jumped up, pulled on his pants and got us each a piece of fish line and some hooks. I was excited too, and yelled, "Hey, Dick, what are you using for bait?" "Grasshoppers," he yelled back at the same time as another fish went sailing over his head and lay flopping on the grass behind him.

"Grasshoppers, of course! I should have known that," I thought. They were easy to catch, not having gotten fully warmed up yet from the morning sun. In a matter of minutes Paul and I each had a long flexible willow pole cut, had trimmed the leaves off and had started to catch fish, letting out a yell equal or louder than Dick's each time. Before we quit we had caught thirty two fish. They were Eastern brook trout and averaged around six or eight inches long. Paul caught the biggest one and it must have been close to twelve inches. "Look at this, will you just look at the size of that fish! Boy, isn't he a beauty?! That was probably the biggest fish in the creek." And on and on. I had to laugh at his excitement and joy, because after all, a fish is a fish.

"Let's get a fire going, so we can eat them," said Paul. "O.K., you guys, start cleaning the fish and I'll start the fire. Then I'll come help you finish." As I said this, both of them just stood there looking at me. "What's the matter?" I asked. "One of you can build the fire and I'll clean the fish, I don't care," thinking maybe this was the trouble.

Dick then said, "Slim, it's not that. Paul nor I have never cleaned a fish in our whole life." After I showed them how to clean fish and we had fried them for our breakfast, we ate all but three. We had eaten fish until we just couldn't eat anymore. They were delicious being firm and fresh from the cold water. Paul ate his big one and insisted that Dick and I taste it to see for ourselves how much better it tasted than the others.

After we finished eating they told me their story and I found out that as far as this part of the country was concerned there was very little else that they knew about the west. Paul said he had an uncle who was supposed to be living in the big city I had left. He and Dick both lived in Pennsylvania and about a month ago they had bought this car and had come out west for the adventure and planned to end up at the uncle's house. Their planning hadn't gone any further than the Uncle because they expected him to take them in, give them a place to stay and help them find jobs. There was nothing wrong with that and everything would have gone according to plan, except, when they got to the Uncle's last known address, he had moved and no one could tell them where.

So here they were, more than two thousand miles from home, almost broke apparently unable to find jobs and worse, probably couldn't hold them if they did. Paul then said, "We're sure glad we had to stop and put water in the radiator of the car and found you. Maybe you can help us." I thought to myself, " Isn't life funny." Last night I would have given anything to be just like they were and join them so that I could have some company for awhile. I really needed them, and now this morning, it turned out that they needed me, and it looked like they needed me even more than I needed them.

"Well yes, I'll help you. Let's gather up all our junk and hit the road. We'll find a job doing something." I said this with a little more confidence than I felt, because, while I was sure I could always find a job, finding three of them might be different. But, in the meantime I had two friends, was going down the road in a car, instead of walking and we were all young, and full of fish. All in all, I felt things could be much worse and certainly had been just two days before.

The old car chugged along almost as if it had a mind of its own. It refused to be hurried and if whoever was driving got impatient, it simply heated up and the escaping steam from the radiator cap let us know it was about to blow its top. As soon as we slowed down it would cool off and everything would be fine. I was sure that if it had been able to talk its comment would have been, "All right boys just take it easy. I've been doing this for a long time and I'll get you there."

Of course, that was the big question. I had no idea where to go or what to do when we got there. Dick and Paul were perfectly happy having found someone to solve this problem for them; and seemed to be sure that I could do it. So I figured I'd better come up with something. We had been traveling for some time through what must have been an immense valley. On each side of the highway were fields that appeared to end at the foot of mountain ranges far in the distance. Paul asked, "What is all that stuff growing in the fields?" This was one question I could answer and I told him, "It's fields of alfalfa, and we must be in cattle and sheep country, because alfalfa is planted for their feed." Not only did I know what it was but I could also tell by the looks of it that it was about ready to be cut.

In the distance on the right side of the road was a large white house. It was the only house for miles and was obviously the center of a great ranch. "Paul," I said, "turn in at that place and let's try our luck." The lane leading to the house was more than a half mile long, bordered on each side with almost mature alfalfa fields. Pulling into the yard, our arrival was greeted by the typical uproar of two barking dogs. This noisy greeting brought a man from the house. He was lean and well built with a face burned to an almost bronze color from exposure to the sun. Cautioning Paul and Dick to keep quiet, I got out to meet him. "Hi" I said, "looks like the hay is about ready to cut. I was wondering if you could use some good help?" "It's not ready and we won't start for about a week", he replied. "If you want to come back then, I could sure put you to work."

"Well, look, we're broke and this is just about as far as we can go. We're out of grub, almost out of gas and we just have to find a job." All this wasn't completely true, but gaining a little sympathy never hurts. "Couldn't you find something we can do just for our food until you start cutting?" This caused him to look at me thoughtfully for a minute, then finally he shrugged and said, "O.K. throw your bed rolls on a bunk in the bunkhouse over there," pointing to a long low building, and "I'll find something for you to do." Dick and Paul were completely happy and carried their blankets into the bunkhouse with a lot of shouting and laughter. Then they told me in loud voices what a great guy I was, how smart I had been in getting us jobs so easily; and how lucky they had been in finding me. I accepted all this gracefully, just like it was deserved, yet at the same time I was already starting to worry. Sure I had talked us into jobs. In a week's time or less this job would be knowing how to harness a team, and hook it up to a mowing machine or a hay rake. I knew I could do any of these things, practically with my eyes shut. I knew also that my newly found friends didn't know one end of a horse from the other. "Oh well, what the hell?" I thought, at least we had a place to eat for a week or so and in the meantime, maybe I'd get a chance to teach them something." At the Jacksons and the other farmers, the horses we had used were well broken and were no problem in doing the work necessary.

To complicate things even further, in this vast country wild horses would be rounded up only at haying time. Most of them had never had a harness put on them and would go crazy with fear and were as mean as hell. The only way to make them work was to blind-fold them, hook them up with an older well-broke horse, then hook that team up to a mowing machine. Then they were worked together until the wild horse settled down from exhaustion. He had no other choice.

As it turned out we didn't even last until the haying started. We had been put to work digging fence post holes, setting the posts, hauling hay for the many horses along with other simple chores that needed to be done. I was able to handle the necessary harnessing and unharnessing of the team we used, and even taught Paul and Dick a little at the same time but it was perfectly obvious to the ranch foreman that they didn't know a damn thing about this work. On the fifth day, after we had eaten breakfast he called me over and said, "Slim, we're going to start haying in the morning. If you want to stay I can use you, but I don't want your partners." What a hell of a note this was. I did want to stay because I needed a job, yet finding these two friends had been the greatest thing that had ever happened to me and I just couldn't give it up so soon. "Well thanks anyway" I said, "but I guess if they have to go I'll go too." Paul and Dick halfheartedly told me to stay, but I could see they were a little scared of being alone again. "The hell with it" I told them. "Let's load up and hit the road." We had already swiped enough gas from the big tank by the barn to completely fill our gas tank. Also, one of our jobs had been to dig spuds, getting enough ahead to feed the large haying crews which would be coming in. We promptly stole two sacks of these potatoes and hid them under our blankets and stuff in the back seat.

So here we were going down the road with a full tank of gas and two sacks of spuds. We've managed to eat well for five days, so all in all it looked like we were ahead. The next job we got was picking hops. These blossoms were used to make beer. Anyone could pick the damn things and maybe some families could make money at it. We sure didn't. We were paid three cents a pound, and if we worked hard and stayed with it, we could gather something like sixty pounds apiece in a day's time. The blossom was light and fluffy and I'm sure it must have taken at least a million of them to weigh sixty pounds. In a week's time though, we had a pretty good stake so we quit. One good thing about us was that we didn't need much money. Gas was cheap, and with a little food, we could get by. Of course that included eating a lot of potatoes.

Anyway, the hop picking had become a losing proposition. Lots of transient families moved in just to pick the hops and other seasonable crops, then when they went back home they were able to live comfortably on the money they had earned. The only trouble, as far as we were concerned, was that in some of these families there were girls. Some young and many older and even married. These women, logically so, could see no reason to stand in the hot sun for two or three hours picking hops, when they could earn the same amount of money or more just by lying on their backs for five minutes in the shade of a hop row. Their price was anything they could get from twenty five cents to a dollar. Since it seemed like all of us had a continuous hard on, we couldn't resist; plus the fact that they were beautiful things, especially the young ones. Paul was the worst and Dick and I finally had to take all his money away from him. The day we quit we found that Paul had traded his whole morning's pickings for a piece of ass. She was a pretty dark eyed girl, not over fifteen years old. But still it had become a choice between screwing or eating. Even I had to admit it was a terrible choice to have to make.

How lucky we were. We landed a job on an extra gang with the railroad company.

It has to be one of the meanest jobs in the world. We were called gandy dancers and I think the name came from the fact that a flat shovel was used, its blade eight inches wide and about a foot long.

As new railroad ties were placed or when the rail was raised to make the track level, the gravel or ballast had to be worked under the tie with these shovels. We would spend all day working gravel under the rail by raising the shovel with both hands then forcing the gravel under the tie with our foot on the top of the blade. I guess anyone looking at twenty or thirty men strung out in a line all raising one foot or the other in unison could imagine that it looked like some crazy dance. To the guy doing it though, it was monotonous, hard work, especially with the sun beating down on the rails. They got so hot that our hands would blister if you touched them and water would sizzle and pop when dropped on them, just like it does on the top of a stove. We were getting three dollars a day with fifty cents taken out for food. The grub was rough and plain, but plentiful. We were living in bunk cars parked on a siding, way out in the middle of a sagebrush desert. No towns, and no girls, so at this rate it was obvious that we were slowly getting rich.

Paul and Dick were getting homesick and they kept saying, "Come on Slim, Come and go home with us." They kept talking about all the work there was back there. Just last night Dick had said, "Hell Slim, we could get jobs in a factory doing piece work. Why, you would make more money in two days than you're making here in a week." I didn't know what to do. One place was pretty much the same as another to me, and I admit I got excited about the adventure of seeing some of the places I had read and heard about. The big mountain ranges that we would cross, and the plains, rivers and cities that I would see made me decide to go, because after all, what the hell's the difference where I am.

We went to Pennsylvania, my two friends and I; and I did get to see the mountains, the vast plains and the great rivers. We made the trip with nothing more than the timing chain breaking, right in the middle of St. Louis, Missouri. We sat there stopped, wondering what to do, when three Negro teen-age boys came by. One of them asked, "Hey man, what's wrong?" When we explained, they laughed saying, "Give us two dollars. And we'll get you a chain and fix the car." The other two got some tools and had the timing chain cover off by the time the other returned with the chain. In no time the car was fixed with much "b s." between the six of us. When finished, they didn't want to take any money but we insisted on giving them a dollar. If this sounds cheap, that dollar could buy twenty glasses of beer.

Paul asked me to come and stay at his home and they told their parents how I had taken care of them, found them jobs, and that they had asked me to come home with them. There wasn't any more work in the east than in the west and I began to realize that another mouth to feed was becoming a burden for the family. So, even though, they all protested, one day I rolled up my clothes in my old blanket, put the rope over my shoulder and said, "I must go home to the west."

I knew their concern for me was mixed with a sense of relief. They were good parents and the two boys had been good friends to me but now their families were complete and back in order. Their sons were home, and once again I was standing on the outside looking in. This feeling no longer bothered me as much. I no longer felt a need to belong, expect love or have a caring relationship with anyone. This had been a handicap that I could throw aside now and I was beginning to develop a strong sense of independence and self confidence. This feeling was borne out while I trudged down a highway three thousand miles from, maybe not home, but at least a place I was familiar with. I would stick out my thumb for a ride, not knowing or caring where the road went.

I was picked up by a delivery man driving a small truck delivering chocolate powder. He worked out of Hershey, Pennsylvania and his route stopped at the small places that made candy. I would help him and usually got candy as a reward. This was too bad because I had bought some candy bars with my money which I could have saved.

His route ended in Scranton, Pennsylvania, so this was where I ended up. While just walking around the streets, I saw a shabby looking hotel sign that said, " beds 25c" I went in and the manager said I could sleep on the floor without paying.

Several old men staying at the hotel had the same look on their faces and in their eyes as the old men sitting in the pool halls at home had had. Yet the next morning they asked me where I was from, seemed concerned enough about me to show me how to survive in the big city. A couple of them took me to a butcher shop, and then to a day old bread window of a bakery. The butcher had old pieces of bologna or lunch meat already in a box for this purpose. We stood quietly by the door not disturbing the paying customers until the butcher handed us some meat. Begging was a fact of life and both the giver and the taker had found a workable compromise. Panhandling for money was another art they taught me, and believe me, they were professionals. I soon excelled at this because I had heard all the angles used by the hobos at Maud's Café. With my new knowledge combined with being a kid I did pretty well. Sometimes I was even able to share some money with them. But I could never be a beggar, so one morning I found an ad in the paper from a farmer who lived in Jermyn, Pennsylvania. Saying goodbye to all the kindly old men who had helped me, I finally managed to get to this town and to his farm. He had advertised for a middle aged farm hand, but when I told him how much experience I had had, he hired me. He told me that he would pay fifteen dollars a month and board and he expected me to work hard. Winter weather in this country was much different from our winters at home. We had snow and cold but here it was freezing rain that covered everything with a sheet of ice. Even the cows and horses had to be kept in the barns most of the time.

This farmer and his wife had two daughters, one about thirty five or forty years old and the other, two or three years younger. Neither had ever married. The younger sister was a teacher at a small rural school. One of the horses was shod with calks or short spikes on his feet for walking on the ice covered roads. I would hook this horse to the buggy and take her to school, then go after her again when school was out. She liked to talk, so we talked and argued about many things on these trips. She also tried to teach me to play the piano. She would stand behind me, lean against my back, put her arms over my shoulders and try to guide my hands. With all of that, I couldn't concentrate and never did learn. I was never going to be a pianist, darn it anyway; but I did enjoy her teaching methods.

All in all it was a pleasant winter but spring had come and the grass may not be any greener over the hill in Pennsylvania, I knew it is greener in

Idaho. I had my winter's wages and intended to hitchhike and ride freight trains west. The family was concerned about my safety and they insisted on making up the difference between my wages and a bus ticket, plus eating money. This was another nice gesture on their part and I knew I would repay them. The trip home to Idaho was uneventful. Four days and nights just sitting, and looking out the bus window, watching the country unfold from large cities, to the plains and mountains, with many stops in small towns along the way.

It was a chance to talk to the different people who sat by me on the bus. All of them were from different backgrounds, some happy, some worried, most concerned about the trouble our country was in because of the depression, especially those with families. Their situations were becoming desperate. I understood this and was glad I had only myself to worry about, knowing that I could survive. One of the men I met on the bus was from Salmon, Idaho. He had thought there was a good chance of getting a job at the Patterson mine in the Pashimeroi Valley, close to Salmon. His brother was meeting him in Boise to drive him home and he offered to let me ride with them. I had heard about working the mines and that lots of men wouldn't work at any other job. They said that it was cool in the summer and warm in the winter; and anyone who worked out in the hot sun or the cold was crazy. This made sense, so I rode to Salmon with them. The mine wasn't hiring any men but since the first cutting of hay was ready, I became one of the crazy ones and spent days out in the hot sun working in the hay fields. I was paid two dollars a day along with great meals which were provided.

When the haying was finished, I still thought mining would be a good job so I decided to head for the Silver Valley at Wallace and Kellog, Idaho. These mines had produced more silver than any place in the world. Once again, with my bindle over my shoulder, I went out to the edge of Salmon to hitch a ride. There were no railroads or buses coming through this part of the country.

Chapter 5
Sex

Guidance

A third of my life
I've spent on my knees
praying for guidance
and trying to please.

Leaving nothing to chance,
expecting divine intervention
to lesson my strife,
I would weep and wail.

All to no avail.
Finding the devout sinner
seemed to always prevail,
so since I can't seem to win,

I believe I will join in
those wallowing in sin
and have a little fun
before my life is done.

I was lucky, got a ride all the way to Missoula, Montana, got a room for a dollar and treated myself to a good meal. The next morning I again went to the edge of town to catch a ride. It was foolish to start walking because of the many miles of nothing, not even many towns. While I was sitting on my bedroll waiting for a ride, a girl about my age came walking by, and made a remark about my being too lazy to stand up to hitch a ride. She walked across the road and stood on a bridge looking down at the water. I walked over and we got to talking. She said she had been working in Missoula all summer, but lived in St. Maries, Idaho and was going home. She planned to buy a bus ticket the next day. I made the remark that it was too bad she didn't hitchhike with me and save her bus fare. I had no idea that she would agree to this but she got all excited, thinking it would be fun, and asked me to wait for her while she hurried back a short distance to the bus station for her suitcase.

When she returned, I suggested she try to thumb a ride while I stayed out of sight, pointing out that a pretty girl had a much better chance of getting a ride than both of us. She readily agreed, and it was not long before a truck screeched to a stop to pick her up. When I walked out carrying her suitcase the two men in the cab were obviously disappointed but opened up the back of the empty truck to let us in. In the truck was a large air mattress which was a bed for the relief driver to sleep on. The highway went through Coeur d'Alene, Idaho with St. Maries about forty miles south. The drivers were probably glad to get rid of us, especially me. I had ruined their day. It wasn't too far from Missoula to Coeur d'Alene, but we had time to get acquainted. She liked to talk, so I didn't have to say much. Mostly she hated to go home. Hers was a large family, with never enough money. Her dad drank and so on and so on. But she also thought I was smart for saving her some money, and wished she could show her appreciation. I had been thinking of a way, but after my experience with Mary, I was afraid to make the suggestion.

However, as we got closer to Coeur d'Alene, with her lying next to me on the mattress giving me a squeeze and an occasional kiss, there was no doubt that I was going to stay with her. I got us two rooms at a hotel for two dollars a day, thinking she would want some privacy. We had no more than gotten into our rooms, when she knocked on my door and asked if I would help pull her boots off. The next morning I gave up my room. It was the sensible thing to do as I would save two dollars a day. Coeur d'Alene was a pretty place on the edge of a large, beautiful lake, surrounded by mountains and pine trees. She let her folks know she was all right, so we spent almost a week going to shows, riding the cruise boat around the lake and eating good food. Our room had a large picture window, looking out over the lake, so we spent a lot of time in the room, where I never tired of looking at the scenery spread out before me, and I even occasionally looked out the window.

I was going broke so when she asked me to go to St. Maries with her, I bought two bus tickets. When we got to St. Maries, she went home. I never saw her again. I had spent over a month working out in the hot sun and if you had asked me, "Was it worth it?" I would have said "yes". I suspect that many men have spent a lot more for a lot less.

Chapter 6
I Am a Cowboy

Mortals

Row upon row they stand
countless, like the grains of sand
stretching on into infinity
with still plenty of room left
for such as you and me.

And as someone once so wisely said,
"What fools we mortals be".

Do any of us pause and reflect
about our life in circumspect?
To that endless row of souls
once a human form also
with hopes and dreams and goals
that have long since
become insignificant.

Through the town of St. Maries runs a mainline railroad. Since I was sleeping down by the tracks I saw that a passenger train called the Portland Rose, stopped occasionally to either pick up or let off a passenger. One day when it stopped, I climbed on the back of the engine. It turned out to be a terrifying ride. The train was traveling eighty or ninety miles per hour; the wind was full of dust, and smoke and swirled around in my space like a tornado. With the dust choking me and the wind about to blow me off, I was really scared. Behind the engine was a baggage car. It had a small space about two feet deep and the front of that opened into a door at the end of the baggage car. I saw, when the train went around a sharp curve, the space between the engine and the baggage car opened up on one side. The next time that it felt like we were going into a sharp curve, I took a deep breath and slipped into the opening. That was much better, at least I couldn't be blown off. After two or three hours during, which time I even took a little nap, the train stopped. One of the train crew walked by the engine with an oil can oiling the wheels. What a time to have to sneeze, but I couldn't control it. In hearing this, he spotted me, and in no uncertain words told me to get the hell out of there. But I couldn't get out, because when the train stopped the space had closed up. The engineer now joined the oiler and they were upset because they had to open the side door, and then the end door, to let me out. My weight hadn't slowed their train down any, but I think they couldn't understand why I hadn't been killed, and only wanted to see me on the ground and in one piece and out of their sight.

We had stopped in a vast wheat country with rolling wheat fields as far as you could see, and a narrow two lane highway winding off into the distance. I was one dirty boy with black coal smoke in my ears, up my nose and probably other places as well. I went into a service station restroom and after about three sinks of black water finally got cleaner. After eating a hamburger and a milkshake, things began to look better.

I stood at the edge of town and it wasn't long before an old battered pickup stopped. A Mexican man and his wife were in the cab, couldn't speak English, but motioned me to get in the back. I wondered where I could sit as the back of the pickup was full of kids of all ages. They made room for me, and it sure beats walking. The kids smiled and looked at me. One said something in a beautiful sing-song voice and they all laughed. They were a happy bunch. One of them said, "You Gringo", so what ever that was, I must have been one. After several hours we arrived in Pendleton, Oregon and this was where they let me off. I thanked the parents and as they drove away the kids yelled, "Adios Gringo". I still don't know what I was.

Pendleton was located in a long narrow valley on the west side of the Blue Mountains. Even though I still had a little over three dollars I managed to get a good meal by washing dishes in one of the restaurants. I was glad also, to hear train whistles, so when I finished washing dishes, I walked down to the tracks. There was the usual jungle where the hobos congregated, so I spent the night and felt quite at home.

The next morning I found out this was the Oregon short line and actually went over the Blue Mountains and through Nampa, Idaho, not far from where I had lived. I had been gone for almost three years and during this time I had found there were many worse things than what I had experienced in Idaho. Besides it was the only place I have to go and I had to find a place to stay for the winter. All the box cars were loaded with freight headed inland from the western seaports with not an empty box car on the train. One flat car was loaded with long bridge timbers twelve and fourteen inches square. They were about twenty feet long and covered the whole car, except for one corner where a few shorter timbers had left a small space about eight feet square. Most hobos would not ride the trains unless they could get inside a car, but I and a man in his mid-fifties got on this corner and leaned up against the timbers. The fall weather was mild so it wasn't too bad.

The long freight train was slow moving because of the full box cars and the long grades climbing into the mountains. We rode all day and had finally reached the summit by evening. I had bought a loaf of bread and a roll of bologna, which I shared with the man who had gotten on with me in Pendleton. He was a carpenter, returning from a job to his home in southern Idaho. The top of the Blue Mountains levels out for several miles so the train picked up some speed. This was good, but it also created a cold wind to our exposed end of the flat car. The night time temperature had dropped and we were getting quite cold. I had been clinching my jaws shut so long that they ached. Clearly something had to be done, or we were going to freeze to death. When we finally stopped for the steam engine to take on water, we saw an old shack close to the tracks. The carpenter had his tool box, so we quickly ripped off some of the 1 x 12 boards from the old shack, and with a few nails built a lean-to off the end of the bridge timbers. This gave us a small room, out of the wind and probably saved our lives. We finally got to Nampa, Idaho where I got off. I waved goodbye to my companion as he continued on his way in the little house we had built.

Evening had come and I was hungry and very cold. A small concrete building was next to the tracks and was an engine room of some kind. It had a large tank and some type of engine that would run off and on. It was warm in the building so I crawled in behind the tank, rolled out my blanket on the concrete floor and got a good night's sleep. Years later I found the small concrete building abandoned, but it was the place where I had spent the night.

It was sure good to be back in the Boise valley. In all my travels I had never seen a place that looked as good. I suppose it was just being able to look up at the familiar Boise Front, the streets and buildings. While walking around town, I met a farmer who had known me when I worked in the hayfields for the Jacksons. He remembered me and wanted to know about my travels and what I had been doing. When I said that I had just gotten back and was looking for a job, he asked if I would feed his cattle during the winter. This was really a stroke of luck, as winter was coming and I sure needed to find something. His name was Mr. Leo Martins and his ranch house was at the end of North Meridian Road. It was a large white house, sitting on the rim. The house where I stayed is still there. Below the rim he had about two hundred head of Black Angus cattle. It was a good job. All I had to do was to load a wagon with hay, then drive down a road off the rim and scatter the hay across the field for the cattle to eat. I did this twice a day. In between times, there was very little to do.

There was an old car behind the barn which was not being used and when I asked about it, Mr. Martins said it still ran. He sold it to me for twenty dollars. It needed some work, a new battery and lots of cleaning up but it did run. I drove by the place where I used to live with the Jacksons, but even though I accepted his needs with more tolerance, I still couldn't stop to see them. The hurt was still there. I wanted to see my friend Rod and his sister Ellen, but they had moved and no one knew where they had gone. I was sorry because Rod had been my only childhood friend and Ellen had been my first love.

That winter was severe with much snow and extreme cold. In the pasture where I had fed cows, there were several small ponds, fed by seepage from the river. Hundreds of different kinds of ducks landed on these ponds; but that winter the weather was so bad that they couldn't find feed because of the snow. Starving, the ducks began to feed at the fish hatcheries, which caused screening to be placed over the fish ponds to keep the ducks from eating the young fish. As the ducks got weaker they could not paddle fast enough to keep the water in the ponds from freezing and they simply froze to death in the ice. Ducks died by the thousands that winter.

One day while I was in town I saw a girl who used to ride on the make-shift bus that took us to high school. We started talking about the past and she was very interested in where I had been and what I had done. I asked her if she would like some ice cream or a milkshake. She said she would like that, so we went into an ice cream parlor. We sat and just talked for almost an hour. She had raven black hair and beautiful brown eyes and I begin to revise my opinion of blondes.

Lorraine

Even though it was the first time we had been together it was easy for us to talk to each other. Never before had I sat down with a girl who seemed interested in me just for who I was. When I asked her if she would like to go with me to a picture show sometime she smiled and said, "Yes that would be nice". I think I'm in love and her name is Lorraine.

The hard winter was ending and now the cows were having their calves. Hereford cattle are red with a white face, but these were Black Angus and most are completely black, except a few that have a white face also. One of the prettiest sights in the world is a bunch of baby calves frolicking around in a pasture. They run with their tails up or bounce around stiff-legged like a rubber ball. The cows with their first calves would run after their babies with anxious looks on their faces like, I suppose, all new mothers do, animal or human. The older cattle would lie down, peacefully chewing their cud knowing full well that when they were ready to stand up and give a quiet moo, the calf would come running to get some milk. They were fun to watch.

Lorraine and I date occasionally. I didn't understand why, but I did know that I felt comfortable with her, and hoped she continued to let me take her places. Mr. Martins also owned a ranch about fifty miles from here and it was time to drive the cattle and the new calves to this ranch in the mountains for their summer pasture. Lorraine didn't know that she had become my true love and when I told her goodbye, I said that I would be back. I was to go on the drive and my job was to take the same team of horses I had used all winter, which were now hitched to a sheep wagon.

This wagon had a canvas top, a wood burning stove, cupboards and was designed as a home for a sheep herder who would spend all summer, along with his dogs, trailing large bands of sheep in the hills.

Chuck wagon of a Basque sheepherder.

Most of the men who herded sheep were Basque, who came from a small country on the north central part of the Iberian Peninsula and on the southwestern edge of France. The Basque are a hardy, proud people. They were hard working and completely trustworthy; and willing to put up with the lonely herder's life. They were excellent herders. Many would take a few head of sheep as part wages, and eventually ended up owning more sheep than their employers. I believe, that, Boise, Idaho had the largest concentration of Basque families in the United States.

I was excited about going on a cattle drive and early one morning we started out. The cattle were restless as they left the pasture, but finally settled down and were all strung out, with me bringing up the rear. I learned that there was always one old cow who had made the trip many times. A bell would be put around her neck and with each step it would ring. She led the way and all the rest followed her. The cowboys kept them headed in the right direction, but sometimes had to chase a stray back to the herd. Late in the afternoon we stopped close to a stream so the cattle could drink and graze on the fresh new grass. Soon, they would bed down for the night.

We will use our wagon as a chuck wagon and I will do the cooking for the cowboys driving the cattle. There were three cowboys and one of them was named Dutch Doty. He owned a pretty little buckskin horse with a black stripe down its back. The other two men were brothers who lived near Meridian. I learned how to use the stove and could turn out a pretty good meal. Plenty of strong black coffee, along with bacon and eggs for breakfast; good ham sandwiches for lunch as the herd, and cowboys kept moving; and we had an assortment of canned foods, along with steaks, potatoes and gravy for supper. So, as I had read about in western stories, I was now driving a chuck wagon on a cattle drive. Chuck wagon is the true name for this vehicle. I don't know where the name came from, but I guess food could be called chuck. Either that or with an amateur cook like me, maybe the cowboys will take a few bites and chuck it.

I had cooked our supper and made a big pot of coffee, then we made a nice fire to sit by. Looking into the fire listening to the cowboys talk, with an occasional moo from one of the cows calling her calf, created such a mysterious primitive feeling that it was as though you could visualize your ancestors staring into the flames. They would have nervously seen the eyes of wild animals reflected in the fire light, who would have liked to make a meal out of them; but the fire kept the wild animals at bay. Finally we rolled out our bedrolls and every thing became quiet. I lay looking up at the stars that seemed close enough to touch. While lying there dosing, I was halfway dreaming about Lorraine, and the next thing I knew it was morning.

The first thing I did was make a full pot of coffee. It was strong and black. Then I had breakfast ready by the time the cowboys had saddled their horses, gotten the cattle up, so they could feed for awhile, and get a good drink of water. The cattle were used to traveling and they strung out and followed the bell without any trouble. That evening was the same as before and we planned to reach the ranch by tomorrow afternoon. The next day one of the cows died, leaving her calf without a mother. One of the cowboys said it happened; animals are no different than people. They get old and tired, so this was, to be her last trip. I felt sorry for the baby, but he picked her up, and put her across his lap and the saddle. When I asked what would happen to the calf, he smiled and said, "I believe you're gonna' find out".

The boss was at the ranch when we arrived with the cattle, and had the gate open to a large meadow of several hundred acres. The meadow was completely fenced where the cattle and calves would spend the summer. The boss asked me if I would stay and take care of the place and since we liked each other and the wages were good, I agreed to stay. The cowboys loaded their saddle horses into a truck, told me I was probably the worst cook they had ever had, laughed, said goodbye and headed back home. The orphan calf had been put in the barn and was plaintively bawling for its mother and something to eat. A gentle milk cow was kept at the ranch for milk to drink, and also to feed an orphan calf if necessary. I milked the cow, put some milk in a bucket, put the baby calf's mouth in the milk, stuck my finger in her mouth to suck on and soon taught her to drink from the bucket.

There were some horses at the ranch and the boss and I saddled up two of them and rode all the way around the fenced meadow. My job was to do this each day, making sure the fence was in good repair. He had also brought a good cattle dog, so when he left I was alone with a couple hundred cattle and calves, one smart dog named Jake, one dumb heifer calf named Babe with me, somewhere in between the two. The ranch house had a kitchen, well stocked with food, running water piped from a spring, two bedrooms with good beds and even a battery powered radio. Light was provided by a Coleman lantern that used white gas, and when pumped up gave off a good white light.

There were a lot of old magazines, like the Saturday Evening Post, Liberty, and many others. There were also some books. One that I especially liked was, *Riders of the Purple Sage* by Zane Gray. For the first time in my life I had a chance to just sit and read, and I found I enjoyed it very much. The ability to string words together and create a story is fantastic. Words are fun, and when I see a word I attempt to understand its meaning, then file it away in my mind. I read aloud to Jake and he, being man's best friend would thump his tail with great enthusiasm and approval.

Each morning I fed Babe, saddled up one of the horses, then Jake and I would check the fence around the pasture. I also carried a 30-30 carbine rifle in a saddle scabbard, just in case there should be a coyote or mountain lion bothering the cattle. This was not likely, as a mother cow will take on anything in defense of her calf. The place was called the Squaw Creek Ranch and got its name from a large mountain that, from a distance, looked like an Indian woman's head. From the mountain ran a cold clear stream which naturally was called Squaw Creek It ran through the pasture and had excellent trout fishing. The boss brought up fresh supplies each weekend and since he loved to fish and ride around looking at his cattle, he would sometimes stay, letting me take the pickup back to town. I stayed at his home place where I had spent the winter, and would call Lorraine for a date whenever I was in town. Usually she would go with me to a show or roller skating.

Lorraine was a kind person and I worried that maybe she was only going out with me to avoid hurting my feelings, because she knew that I was an orphan. Whatever her reason we did seem to enjoy each other's company. I also enjoyed the solitude of the ranch, liked my job, and was good friends with Jake the dog, Babe was getting bigger each day and had even learned to eat grass. All in all, I was happier than anytime before in my life. The summer passed, with only one hard working week, when all the calves had to be branded with the S.Q., the registered Squaw Creek Brand, and the bull calves had to be castrated. During that week the cowboys came back with their horses, and rounded up all the cattle and then separated the calves from their mothers. A fire was built, allowed to burn down to a hot bed of coals, and a half dozen branding irons were put into the fire to get red hot. The cowboys would rope a calf, drag it bawling and bucking to the fire where it would be grabbed, thrown on its side and the hot iron burned the letters S.Q. onto its hip. If it was a bull calf its bag holding the testicles would be slit, the cord to the testicles cut and the testicles tossed into a wash tub. The wound was then treated with disinfectant to keep flies off and stop any infection. The calf was then let up. All of this was done in a choking dust, the smell of burning hair and a chorus of crying calves and bawling mothers.. It was hot dirty work, and I enjoyed every minute of it. Some of the wives had come up with their cowboy husbands, and cooked up huge meals, which were surely needed. One of the main courses were the testicles that had been cleaned, then deep fried in large Dutch ovens. They were called Rocky Mountain oysters and were quite good. I had read once that if you ate an enemy's heart, you gained his strength. I wondered if the bull calf's testicles would have the same effect on the older men. One thing for sure, I didn't need them.

Mr. Martins asked me to work for him in his mill at a place above the ranch, called High Valley. It was run by Mr. Martins' son, Leo Jr. It was a well equipped saw mill with a large steam engine that turned a fly wheel. Connected to this large fly wheel was a ten inch wide belt which was around another wheel, that turned a large circular saw, which sawed the bark off the side of the log. It was then flipped over by steam driven arms until all four sides of the log were removed, leaving a square block of the tree. This square block would again travel through the saw which cut slabs of board, either one inch or two inches thick, depending on the amount of knots. The knot amount would determine the grade of the finished lumber, either #1, #2, or if poor quality, #3.

The rough slab was then dropped on a flat table equipped with smaller, movable saws that could be set to cut the best size of lumber with the least amount of waste, such as 2 x 4s, 2 x 6s, 2 x 10s and so forth. I worked there almost a month before going back to the ranch. Young Leo wrote me a check for $90.00, which I didn't have a chance to cash until we took the cattle back to the home ranch. When I did try to cash it, the bank said it was worthless, due to insufficient funds. I could have gotten the money from his father, but he was a fine man and I wouldn't be the one to let him know that he had a crooked son.

The rest of the summer passed and it was time to trail the cattle back to the home place for the winter. The calves had grown big and no longer needed their mother's milk. Babe became just another one of the herd. I had decided that I didn't want to feed cattle another winter, thinking a warm mine would still be a good place to work. When I told the boss I was going to quit, he said he was sorry to see me go, and that I had been a good worker. He praised me for having done my job in all kinds of weather without complaining, and said that if he could ever help me, or if I needed a job to come and see him. I was surprised that doing my job to the best of my ability seemed unusual to him because all I had ever known was to do what I was told, as far back as I could remember. At two bucks a day, after a year with very little expense, I had over five hundred dollars in the bank; so I traded for a better car, bought some new Levi pants, shirts, shoes, a hat and spent money lavishly on Lorraine, milkshakes, candy bars and a nice sweater as a present. I told her I was gong to work in the mines because I could be in out of the cold and make more money. She seemed concerned that it was too dangerous, didn't want me to get hurt, and hoped that I

would call her when I was in town. I was still confused about our relationship. I couldn't believe her feelings were any more than friendship. But she
was the only living human being who seemed to care about me; she was all
I had.

CHAPTER 7
ATLANTA AND SILVER CITY, IDAHO

TIME

Time is of the essence.
It can't be held in suspense,
waiting for profound observations,
governed by analytical discretion,
before finally making a decision.

When you someday make up your mind
unfortunately you inevitably find,
you've already fallen behind.
And then because of the years
regardless of shed tears,
life has not been kind.

So, don't dwell in sorrows
you've used up all your tomorrows.
It's too late now to atone
for the "ifs" and "Why didn't I's".
Every man eventually dies
and inherits the same headstone.

Some small, some large in size
dictates the timid from the wise.
Still all are just as dead
and just as soon forgotten.
Though one may rest in silk
or the other in cotton,
the body of each becomes, equally rotten.

Atlanta, Idaho is a small mining town about ninety miles from Boise. The road followed the middle fork of the Boise River and was narrow, rough and in some places hung on the side of a mountain with hundreds of feet almost straight down to the river. When I finally got there I had no idea how to go about getting a job. I found out there was a hiring hall and that anyone wanting work had to be there each morning. This was called rustling. I guess the term comes from the word rustle, such as rustle up a meal or rustle up a job. I have always associated the word with stealing cattle.

I made arrangements at the Greylock Café, the only restaurant in town, to sign my name on my meal tickets until I was hired. The same arrangement was followed at the boarding house. If a man hit town broke and most did, it was the only way he could stay until getting a job. Most working men those days had dignity and were honest. Very little money was lost, as the first thing most of them did when they got paid was to settle up their accounts.

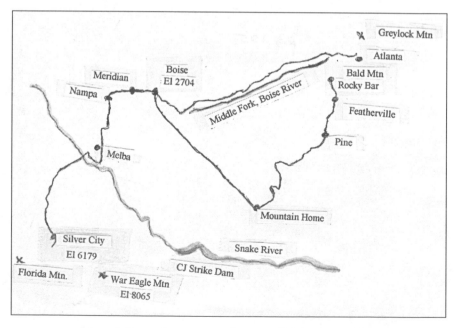

Map of the roads going to Atlanta and Silver City, Idaho

After about two weeks, I was hired as a mucker. A mucker was the person who shoveled the broken rock blasted from the face of the tunnel, which was called muck. Muckers were assigned to work with experienced miners and were expected to help in all parts of the mining process. I was assigned to one of the meanest S.O.B.s you could imagine. He had been a hard rock miner all of his life. Hard rock miners always worked in a mine tunnel, as compared to miners working outside at a placer claim or panning gold from a creek. I was to find that in between his cussing, most of it directed toward me, that I was getting a good education on how to work in a mine. We worked at the end of the tunnel called the face. This had to be drilled with air hammers in a certain way in order to break the rock so that the sides and height of the tunnel would be straight. The pattern of drill

I'm in the center.

holes was very important, usually starting with four holes drilled in an eighteen inch circle. Then another hole was drilled in the center of the circle with holes drilled along each side and across the top and bottom of the face of the tunnel.

This was where experience came in as he could read the hardness of the rock and load the holes with just the proper amount of dynamite. The circle of holes was loaded first, leaving the hole in the center of the circle empty. Then the sides and top were loaded, with the bottom holes loaded last with a much larger amount of dynamite. The dynamite sticks were about twelve inches long and an inch in diameter. The sticks were slit along each side with a knife, placed in the holes and tamped firmly in place with a wooden pole. The slits allowed the stick to crunch when it was packed tightly. One stick was inserted with a blasting cap, which was crimped onto the end of a length of fuse. One of these primed sticks was then pushed gingerly into each hole with one last slit stick of powder to hold it in place.

Now came the crucial part. Each fuse had to be cut to the exact length to explode in sequence, starting with the circle first. The dynamite had to expand outward or it would just shoot back out the end of the hole. This was why the center hole was left unloaded, so there was space to expand outward.

The fuses for all the center holes were cut the shortest, in order to detonate first, then in sequence the right side, the left side and the top. The bottom holes were loaded quite heavily and were called the lifters, and would detonate last. They were called lifters because they would lift the rock upward and out away from the face. The fuses were lit, and we hurried out of the tunnel, with me considerably in the lead toward the fresh air. It was important to count the blasts so we knew that all of the dynamite had detonated, to avoid picking into a blasting cap still in a stick of dynamite, which would be hazardous to your health. The blasting was always done at the end of our shift, so that the smoke and fumes could clear out by morning.

4th Blast: All detonate at the same time

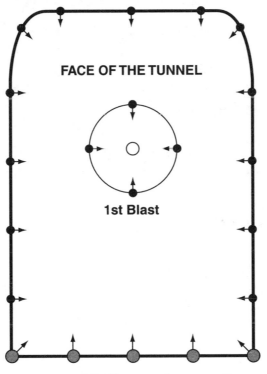

FACE OF THE TUNNEL

3rd Blast:
All of
Left side

2nd Blast:
All of
Right side

1st Blast

5th Blast: All Lifters at the same time

Empty Hole   Loaded Hole   Extra Powder

Planks had been laid on the tunnel floor for the blasted rocks to land on. My job as a mucker was to push a mine car along the tracks to the pile of rock, and with a flat square point shovel load this muck into the car, push it out of the tunnel and either dump it in the waste dump or if it had ore, dump it into a chute to be hauled to the crushers. This was the routine I followed day after day all winter. It was hard work; but I was young and strong, and even though the hard-nosed miner cussed up a storm, we had a mutual respect for each other, so he tried to teach me as much as he could. One very important lesson that I learned from him was that after a blast, you needed to take a long rod and tap the ceiling, listening for a hollow sound. This indicated whether or not a particular spot was loose and might fall on your head. Until I got used to the blasting, I would get a hell of a powder headache, from handling the dynamite, but I suppose a chunk of rock falling on your head would most likely be worse.

I did find that the mine was cool in the late summer when I started, and stayed warm in the coldest part of the winter. I began to think I had found the ideal job and wouldn't want to work any place else. The mine was called the Last Chance and the first time I went into the tunnel I felt the name was right, as I thought it might be my last chance to see daylight again.

After a long days work and supper was finished there was absolutely nothing to do in Atlanta except sit in the pool hall and drink a glass of beer. We listened to the many stories told about incidents which had happened in past years. One was about a man who owned a large ranch at the foot of Greylock Mountain just north of town. His family owned one of the biggest breweries in the country, but he was the "black sheep" of the family. It was said that he was paid a monthly sum of money just to stay away from the business. Whenever he came to town, he would set up his company's brand of beer for the house. I developed a taste for this brand of beer and, in remembering those days, have bought it ever since.

Another story told in the pool hall was about Peg-Leg Annie and her experiences in Atlanta and also her attempt to walk over the mountain to Rocky Bar, another mining town fourteen miles south of Atlanta. The Legend of Peg-Leg Annie was in the 1800's when her father, Steve McIntyre, brought her to Rocky Bar as a child, where she spent most of her life. Her father was killed by the owner of one of the area's mines in a street fight. Peg- Leg Annie married at age fourteen, but was soon widowed. She then went to Atlanta , where she operated a rooming house. One spring day in May, Annie and her friend, Mrs. Emma VonLosh, who was known as Dutch Em, started to walk on the snow crust over the mountain to Rocky Bar. The mountain was rugged with a four mile summit and suddenly a fierce blizzard came up. The blizzard lasted three days and some three feet of fresh snow fell on the mountain. After the blizzard was over, the mailman walked up the mountain and found Annie crawling on her hands and knees almost incoherent. Her feet were frozen. She was taken back to Atlanta and a doctor was called from Mountain Home, some 70 miles away, who arrived five days later and had to amputate her legs, just below the knees. Dutch Em froze to death and her body was found many days later.

When Annie recovered she made woolen pads for her stumps and began to do laundry for miners in Rocky Bar for which she was well paid. She also did some bootlegging during prohibition. Annie endured many hardships during her life and finally died of cancer in 1933. She was buried at Morris Hill Cemetery in Boise, Idaho.

Spring had come and I had saved most of my wages. I wanted to see Lorraine, to be on level ground in the Boise Valley again and see what developed. When I announced that I was quitting, that tough, old miner put his arm around me, and I think he almost squeezed out a tear, when we said goodbye. I had worked hard and had always done what I was told. I realized that his cuss words were not directed to me personally but was just his way of speaking. He had taught me well and I felt that now I could hire out as a miner. But, I didn't really know what to do. I was certain of one thing though; I never wanted to see a horse's rear end again while sitting on a hay mowing machine, or milk another cow during the rest of my life.

When I got down to Boise, I called Lorraine. We went to shows and I treated her to hamburgers and milk shakes. We seemed to be able to talk to each other comfortably, but I didn't know if it was kindness on her part or the hamburgers and milkshakes. I know I enjoyed her company very much for whatever reason. Yet, I thought I was seeing too much of her and that maybe I should take off and leave her alone.

My car ran well and I remembered how pretty the country was around Coeur d'Alene and St. Maries, Idaho, so decided to head that way. I will probably never see the girl who traveled with me from Missoula, but the possibility was nice to think about. I also found out that it was nice to have money. I was not rich but I had a reliable car, and had invested in all the necessities of life: a small tent, a good sleeping bag, some basic utensils, a frying pan, some dishes, an ice chest and some fishing equipment. The highway from Boise to northern Idaho followed the river and I spent ten days or so just moseying along, camping by the river, and easily catching enough fish for supper. I laid in my sleeping bag at night listening to the music the river made and drifted off to sleep without a care in the world. I found I had developed a cynical outlook on life and really didn't need or want an association with anyone, except maybe Lorraine. But, I had done the right thing in leaving her alone. Nothing could ever come of our relationship. Having never had any love in my life, I doubted if I would know how to give it anyway.

Finally getting to St. Maries, I found a job in a blister rust program, which was being done by the Forest Service. We were trucked to a camp in the St. Joe National Forest, where we were to pull a bush that was a host plant for some disease which caused damage to the pine trees. What ever this was, it had to spend time on this bush before attacking the trees. It seemed silly to me, but the pay was good.

I got acquainted with a couple of guys who wanted to go to the northwest to work in the timber when this job was finished. They asked me if I wanted to go along. Since they had a four door sedan, I left my car in St. Maries and we took off to the Northwest. We ended up at Pacific Beach, along the coast of Washington state, and got a job in the timber.

Logging yellow pine in Idaho was much different that what was done here. The Idaho timber didn't grow as tall and logs were cut in 12, 14 and 16 foot lengths, which utilized the full tree from the butt to approximately a 6 inch tip. Once the trees were cut, horses were used to skid the logs to a landing where several logs would be loaded onto trucks. Because of the constant rainfall along the Washington Coast, the trees were two or three times as tall as the trees in Idaho and were cut in long lengths to be loaded onto a flat railroad car.

One method of logging in Washington, was to use a Spar Tree. Topping out a spar tree was quite an event and it was a time when all the crew took a break and watched the spectacle. The spar tree stood alone with all the small trees and brush cleared away.

Picutre #1

The limbs up the tree were to be cut off. The men who watched were quiet, while the climber fastened his climbing spurs, his leather belt with a saw and an ax attached, and started his climb. The belt around his waist had a stout rope fastened to each side and went around the tree. It was flipped out and up allowing him to take another step upward, while sawing off the limbs as he climbed upward.

Finally almost reaching the top, which looked like a Christmas tree thirty to forty feet above his head, he cut the top off. Picture #2 shows the climber right after he has finished cutting the top off. As the top broke off, the tree would whip back and forth violently. He was about 300 feet in the air at that point and I could not imagine a person having the courage to do this. He might have gotten a day's wages for two or three hours of work, but he had earned it. His part was finished and now another man, called a high rigger climbed the tree, pulled

Picutre #2

up a large pulley, fastened it to the top of the spar tree, pulled up a cable, threaded it through the pulley, and brought the end of the cable down. The cable was pulled 800 feet or more back into the timber. The purpose of the spar tree was to lift the front end of the log high enough to go over the tops of small trees and stumps.

This was where I came in. As a choker setter, I dug under the huge, fallen trees, threw the choker over the leading end of the tree and under it, and fastened the cable, coming from the donkey engine and through the pulley on top of the spar tree, to the choker.

In picture #3 you can see the donkey engine, a large steam powered engine that turned the drum behind the man in the white shirt. The cable you see from the drum is going to the top of the spar tree, then to the log and fastened to the choker. The log was pulled quite fast and if it were to hit a stump it would have wrecked the whole operation. All of it was fast and dangerous work, but I was proud to be doing a man's job.

Picture #3

I must say, however, that this was miserable country. Almost every morning fog rolled in and wouldn't burn off until about noon. If there were no fog, it rained. One saying I had heard was "You can't see the forest for the trees." I didn't know what it meant at the time but here the trees were thicker than hair on a dog, and you couldn't see anything but the trees unless you looked straight up, and even then it was usually raining. I longed for my beloved Boise Valley where you could see for miles in any direction. But we stuck it out and finally headed back to St. Maries, when the logging ended for the winter. I picked up my car and again headed back down the road toward Boise.

I made the trip down faster than I had coming up, because I really was beginning to miss Lorraine. My resolve to leave her alone had weakened. I don't mean by this that I had ever considered making a pass at her. Prostitutes were available in all logging and mining camp towns, both large and small. Times were hard and this profession provided needed relief for many men, including me. The girls brought in money to help feed their families, but the source had to overlooked. It was a profession and strict health rules had been established. Each girl was required to have a certificate on the wall in the room she used, stating that an examination had been performed certifying that she was free of any venereal disease and she was required frequent checkups. Since their livelihood depended on this certificate you were also examined carefully before being allowed to indulge. The examination consisted of squeezing the penis toward the tip and if the slightest discharge was seen, you were out the door. If you were OK you were washed thoroughly in a pan of warm soapy water, dried with a towel and welcomed with open arms. By then the act took about five seconds, and looked like the fastest way anyone could make money, with a minimum amount of effort. With regard to this last observation, there was something inequitable here. I had spent ten hours in the hot sun for twenty cents an hour, and I don't ever remember even getting kissed, much less anything else. Your two dollars was collected in advance, but for twenty dollars you could spend the night. I did this once, but lost money on the deal, only using up sixteen of my twenty dollars.

Prostitution has never been an accepted lifestyle in America, as it has been in many other countries. The puritan ethics implanted in our society by our forefathers, dictated that all reference to this biological function, both in sight and mind, had to be suppressed in appearance and most certainly in teaching. The work of a prostitute is one of the oldest professions and it served a very necessary function, probably preventing some acts of forcible rape.

Fall was here with winter not far behind, and even though I had enough money saved to spend the winter in Boise, I decided to take a run over to

Silver City. I couldn't resist calling Lorraine to tell her I was back, and that I was going to Silver City to get a job. She sounded disappointed that I hadn't come to see her. Hearing the disappointment in her voice caused me a great sadness. No one had ever cared about me before. How could I believe that anyone did now?

Silver City, Idaho by Marshal Edson, 1997

Silver City was an old mining town that in its day had made several men rich. The silver was found in veins of blue clay, a freak of nature I guess, and was so rich that it could be sent directly to the smelters in Utah without going through the crushing and extraction process. Most of the old town of Silver City is gone by now, but there are enough buildings left to get an idea of what the town used to look like. The Idaho Hotel is in operation and up until recently you could still rent a room. There is a gold coin slot machine in the lobby and a Wells Fargo Stage Line sign hanging over the registration desk. All the buildings in town are weathered and are beginning to take on the look of a ghost town.

The town had a turbulent past because of many fights between rival mining companies. There was trouble also between the miners and management. Due to the continuous fights and illness, the cemetery above Slaughter House Gulch has many graves. Some are enclosed with a wrought iron fence, as this was the custom at that time. During it's boom days, Silver City had several general stores, a couple of meat markets, two hotels, three or four restaurants and a row of quite elegant houses called Virgin Alley. One married man who was discovered there by his wife, was quickly dispatched to the cemetery at Slaughter House Gulch. Justice in Silver City was swift and fair. A miner who had killed another man was tried and sentenced to hang. A grave was dug and he was marched from the jail, hung and buried. There was no sitting on death row for years while going through appeal after appeal. It is too bad that it is not done that way today.

The Silver City mines were fabulously rich with the Poor Man Mine alone, finding ore that assayed at $5000.00 a ton. During 1870 to 1875 this ore produced over four hundred million dollars. One man named Dewey built the Dewey Palace Hotel in Nampa, Idaho and it was one of the most elaborate show places in the west. The town of Silver City was a booming city in the late eighteen hundreds with many Chinese men working in the mines or making a pretty good living panning for gold along the creeks. The mines had pretty much played out by then, but there was still some activity on Eagle and Florida Mountains.

A man named Bryan Brownell from Murphy was in Silver City and asked me if I wanted a job. He said he had taken a lease on the old Trade Dollar Mine on Florida Mountain and needed some miners. There was a cabin near the mine and he hired me, another miner and a cook and stocked the cabin with food. His intention was to clear out one of the tunnels to its end to see if there was any possibility of finding profitable minerals. To do that we had to work our way through fallen rock by loading it into a mine car and pushing it out to the dump. One day while working we came across an ore chute that went down to the main tunnel some hundred feet below the place where we were working. A ladder along the chute seemed to be in good condition, so I filled my carbide lamp with fresh carbide and climbed down.

I'm in the center helping pull supplies to the cabin.

It was spooky and my small carbide light did little to dispel the darkness. The ladder ended at the main tunnel; and I found out later that this tunnel, which was wide enough for two tracks side by side, was drilled entirely by hand. As I have said before, this was a very rich mine, with millions of dollars having been taken out of it. Because of the remoteness of Silver City it was hard to hire men willing to stay through the severe winter months. One solution was to go overseas to places like Wales and hire men, paying their way to Idaho, to work in the mine. These men were nicknamed Cousin Jacks.

The drilling of holes to load with dynamite was done entirely by hand. If one man drilled holes alone, he would use a four pound hammer with a twelve inch handle and was called a single jack. If the hammer used weighed eight pounds it was called a double jack. The terms single jack and double jack are still used today to designate a four pound hammer or an eight pound hammer. Drill steel had a diameter of one inch with eight sides and a flat chisel point. To use it, a man held the steel in his left hand, palm side up and turned it an eighth of a turn each time he hit it. This allowed the chisel point to chip off that amount of rock in the hole. A double jack was used by two men, one on each side, with a third man holding the steel; again, with palms up, turning it each time, as each man struck alternately. Palms were faced up in turning the steel because if the hammer missed, which was seldom, it just knocked the hand away, instead of breaking the knuckles.

I wandered around in the tunnel and found a large room, evidently having been used for a drying room for clothes, as many different types of clothing were still hanging there along with picks, shovels and other material. Again, in talking to some old timers, they said that when a mine was no longer profitable it would be shut down without notice. Everyone was paid off and sent home, period. It was an eerie feeling down there in the main tunnel alone, thinking of all the hard work done by so many men now dead; and I started seeing ghosts and hearing voices. I climbed back up the ladder and hurried out to the sunshine. I had worked hard all that winter, not even going to town mostly because we couldn't even if we had wanted to, as we were snowed in. One day while I was breaking up a rock that was too big to load in the mine car, a piece of the rock flew off striking me in the inside corner of my eye, next to my nose. I was very fortunate because Tom Roch's wife helped me wash it out with a disinfectant. Mr. and Mrs. Roch had been hired by a mining company to watch the town through the winter months and there was no one else to help me. I still have a scar where the rock chip hit me, and I have always felt blessed that she was there. But spring finally came and the roads became passable. I quit my job, stopped in Murphy and picked up a sizable paycheck, and headed for Boise.

When I went to the bank to deposit the check, it turned out to be worthless. The bank suggested that I take it to Maud Henry, the Justice of the Peace in Nampa and file a claim. I did this and an investigation showed that Mr. Brownell had put everything in his wife's name, and there was nothing I or anyone else could do. I swore I was going to get a gun and go collect my money; and was told by the Justice to go ahead if I wanted to spend the rest of my life in jail. Sometimes life can be a bitch! I was still in pretty good shape though on money, so I got a room and called Lorraine. I was pleasantly surprised at how happy she seemed to be to hear from me. She said she had thought about me and had worried about me all winter; and was so glad I was back. "Well, I'll be damned," I thought. It did lift my spirits after being cheated out of a winter's wages, so I took her to dinner. It seemed to me that she had changed from a girl to a beautiful young lady. She was going to graduate from High School and wanted me to come to her graduation and to meet her family.

This whole proposition scared me, and I pointed out to her that I wouldn't know how to act; would be afraid to meet her family, and thought I had talked my way out of it when I said I didn't even have a suit, and had never worn a tie in my life. With this she insisted that I meet her at a clothing store where she would help pick out the appropriate clothing. It looked like I was stuck. We had a lot of fun, with me being self conscious as I tried on different suits, with correct shirts, neckties, shoes and socks to go with the suit. Finally selecting one that she approved of, I was pleasantly surprised at what a fine figure of a man I presented. My self confidence increased tremendously. I stood up proud, preening myself in front of a full length mirror; but the real result of my new glory was seeing a glimmer of admiration in Lorraine's eyes. I was instructed as to how to get to her house, when to get there in time to meet the family, then go to the graduation with them. The closer the time came, the more nervous I got; when I finally arrived, I was welcomed by "The Mother" who was able to ease my fears right away by saying, "What a fine looking young man you are."

Lorraine had an older brother, Louis and an older sister, Mary, both of whom looked me over with a large degree of skepticism; and three younger brothers, who also looked me over, but more out of curiosity than anything else. Her father shook my hand, and either grunted or said humph. I was not too sure about his feelings, but I sensed that if I even thought about associating with one of his daughters I would be in trouble. I did have sense enough though to buy Lorraine a nice bracelet for a graduation gift. Later on when we dated, I found out that her father had a heart condition, caused by the first World War, and periodically had to spend time in the Veteran's Hospital in Boise. He could only work occasionally, and all the rest of the family did what they could to help out. The family had lived in Texas where Lorraine was born. Then they moved to Kansas and finally to Idaho. When they arrived in Idaho in 1935 they were amazed at the fruit that was available, most of it free for the picking, especially if prices were low.

"The mother" was a great woman and had insisted that the family locate near a college, as she was determined that all of her children would become educated. She dedicated her life to this goal. Both Louis and Mary had been attending the College of Idaho, now known as Albertson College of Idaho, a small liberal arts college located in Caldwell, Idaho. Lorraine would start as a freshman in the fall following her graduation. It was obvious I could never fit into this family with it's dedication to education, even though I had graduated fourth highest in my eighth grade class. Please let's leave it at that, without asking how many were in my class.

You can better understand my feelings at that time, by understanding the final outcome of the mother's dedication toward education. As a result of this almost obsession, during the most economically depressed era of our country, her children earned twelve college degrees, six of them from The College of Idaho.

> Louis B. Thomas, BA, MS, MD., Honorary PhD.
>
> Mary Thomas Suhre Miller, BA, Honorary PhD.
>
> Lorraine Thomas Hosac, BA.
>
> Weldon L. Thomas, BA, MD.
>
> Elmer R. Thomas, BA, MS., PhD., Honorary PhD.
>
> Lloyd Thomas, BA., MS., 60 hrs toward PhD.

Her unshakable belief in education has now been carried forth by her children and grandchildren, who have earned a total of 85 college degrees. Grandma Thomas, as she was called in her later years, died on February 11, 1987. She was honored by her children with the establishment of the Louis L. and Maud Alsa Thomas scholarship fund at the College of Idaho. During the Baccalaureate Service in 1987, The College of Idaho honored her, her husband and the Thomas Family.

The mortician who handled the services for Mrs. Thomas, when she died, was supposedly a good friend of mine and made the following comment after the service, "Here were all these doctors and Ph.D's and then came this Polock whom Lorraine married."

CHAPTER 8
LORRAINE AND I MARRY

JUDGEMENT

Observe if you must
with degrees of trepidation
depending on your concern
and personal interpretation,
stemming from love or disgust
of the one under observation.

But attempt to be fair,
in that your final conclusion
of what you think you see
is not based on an illusion
of what you would have them be.
Then, with humility
and, certainly empathy,
accept, what is or isn't there.

This is individual decision,
the only factual criterion
for solving the unknown
short of Heavenly Vision
in judging anyone.
The true sin you may have to atone
is being the one, who casts the first stone.

The more I thought about this distinction between Lorraine and me, the more depressed I became; so I again headed for St. Maries, where I had made friends and knew I could find work. I packed my pretty new clothes in a cardboard box, thinking that I would never wear them again; left them with the landlord where I had my room, and again with a real sense of loss and sadness called Lorraine, told her goodbye, and left town. I had had the pleasure of getting dressed up, watching her graduate, meeting the other skeptical members of her family, especially "The Father" and had accepted the truth, all the while knowing that I loved her hopelessly.

I'm second from the right.

The trip north was uneventful and I soon got a job sawing white pine. Northern Idaho had one of the largest stands of white pine in the nation. It was a two man operation using a crosscut saw with a handle on each end, and I was fortunate to become partners with an expert saw filer. The art of filing saws, which are used in operations from the large saws in saw mills to smaller saws in different trades, was a real talent. Experienced saw filers were specialists and, as such could expect to receive higher than average wages for their abilities.

Filing a saw demanded much more than just using a file to sharpen the teeth. It was also necessary to tap the saw tooth to the proper angle so that the teeth would make a cut wide enough for the saw to slide through the cut in the wood without binding. This part of the filing operation was called swedging and was as important as sharpening the teeth themselves. To file the teeth of a saw and swedge them was a absolute necessity, in order to make the work of sawing easier. And it needed to be made as easy as possible! We climbed up the sides of mountains, with one of us carrying the saw, then felled the trees. We had only to fall them and buck them up into twelve or fourteen foot lengths. Some one else would chop the limbs off and skid them to a landing. For this we earned ten cents per log; and in a thick stand of timber we could make good money. This work was where saw filing became so important, as each time we pulled the saw back and forth through a log, the sharp teeth had to cut easily and sometimes pulled shreds, 4 to 6 inches long, out of the cut. The Ohio Match Company had hired us; and used this soft, clean timber to make wooden matches.

Sitting by our tent.

We had a tent, and I did the cooking while my partner, who was from Iron Mountain, Michigan, did the filing. We stayed out in the woods from Sunday until Saturday night; then we went into St. Maries, to do a little celebrating, recovered Sunday, bought some groceries, and went back early Monday morning to go to work. I think that I must have pulled that damn saw back and forth ten thousand miles at least. But, by the end of the summer we had made some very good money. Even though Lorraine and I had written each other, I still felt there was no point in going back to Boise; so I decided to try again to make it to the Couer d'Alene mining district and spend the winter. I was determined to get there this time, stranded girls or not.

Kellogg, Idaho was the central town from which most of the men were hired to work in the various mines. Times were hard and the line of men looking for work some mornings extended around the block. I was fortunate to have some money and with just myself to take care of. Also, I had my tent, sleeping bag and could cook my own meals. I would remember Maud feeding the hungry, and now found myself also occasionally feeding someone who was broke and hungry. Maud used to say, "Cast your bread upon the water and it will return many fold". I logically doubted this but it didn't cost me much in case she might be right. It took ten days, but I finally got hired and was to work in the Star Morning Mine at Mullan, Idaho

Throughout the west, some of the richest mines in the world were found by accident. Many stories were told about the old bearded prospector wandering around the hills and mountains with his only companion, a donkey that packed all his worldly possessions. Folklore will recount a story that one day the prospector sat down in the shade of an outcropping of rock and idly chipped off a piece and found it full of veins of gold and silver. Some of these tales were actually true; but most were the exception.

The Coeur d'Alene mining district stretches for miles in what is called The Silver Valley, located in northern Idaho

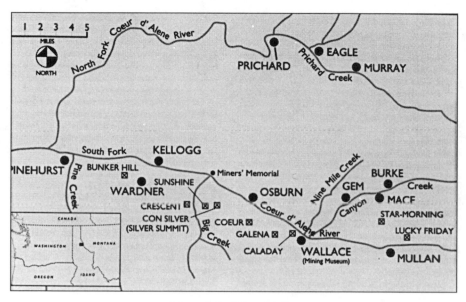

Map of the Silver Valley.

This area was not located by accident. Some of the best geologists and mining engineers in the world were instrumental in determining that it was fabulously rich in silver and also zinc and lead.

I can only attempt to explain the methods used by the many huge mining companies that had been extracting the minerals from this area as far back as 1885. By the mid 1980s almost five billion dollars worth of metal had been produced from these mines. The mining companies were as vast as some industrial areas, as shown in the picture on the next page of the Star Morning Mine, located near Mullan, Idaho.

The town was created by the miners and their families. Many of these miners are third generation and had spent a lifetime working here.

Most of the mines provided what could be called a hotel and was located close to the mine. The single rooms were adequate and the dining room served excellent meals which could be ordered from a menu. This was where the single men stayed. The daily routine was to get up and have a good breakfast, then go to another adjacent building called the drying

The Star Morning Mine

room, where lockers were provided for our clean clothes and our working clothes. The working clothes from the day before hung from hooks that were raised up to dry. I joined the many other men, milling around, waiting to load on the train that would carry us some 9000 feet to the landing. This long tunnel had been dug progressively over the years until reaching a place where the rich veins of ore spread out in all directions. To follow these veins, tunnels angled off from the main tunnel and also stopes were created to follow the rich veins upward. This huge hollowed out area was called the landing. From this initial landing shafts were dug 200 feet down, where another landing would be created. This method was followed every 200 feet with the ore being brought up to the main landing, then taken out to the outside of the mine.

The Star Morning Mine reached a depth of 8000 feet. To get to these 200 foot apart levels, men were loaded onto double decked cages, called skips. The skip held 32 men and dropped at the rate of 600 to 800 feet per minute I was assigned to work in a stope at the 4000 foot level.

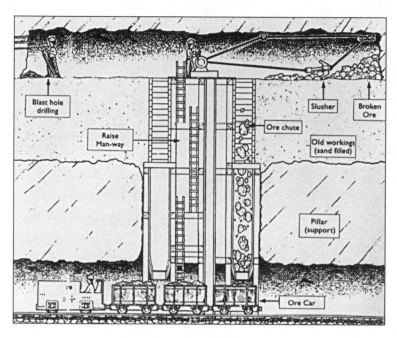

A stope.

The picture shows a man at the left end drilling holes to blast the rock, and at the right end another man running what is called a slusher, dragging the blasted rock to the ore chute and to the mine cars below. Any rock that didn't have profitable ore was called waste and it was used to help build up platforms to work the stope upward. By using the same air which was provided through a hose, we could position a jack leg hammer firmly against the ceiling and the floor and drill holes, using the jack hammer attached to the jack leg. My job was to drill holes with this jack leg hammer. There was also a smaller hose that forced water through a hole in the drill steel, keeping the drilling dust wet. In the old days, the miners drilled

Jack Leg Air Hammer.
Picture from Jerry Dolph's book,
Fire in the Hole

without water, and the dust, would cut their lungs to pieces. This was called silicosis and many men died a lingering death because of this condition. There were no government regulations and certainly no modern day technology or guidelines to follow. These companies and their investors had only one purpose in mind and that was to supply these minerals as economically as possible. To do this, they did exploit the working man by allowing conditions to exist that were detrimental to their health, safety and welfare.

Because of this, the men also took a stand and demanded portal to portal pay. The opening of a tunnel going into a mountain was called a portal. Portal to portal pay meant that the miner's pay started when he entered the tunnel and ended when he exited the tunnel at the end of his shift. Before this, his 9000 foot ride going to the landing, and then out of the mine, was on his own time. They also demanded better air to breathe, hospitals for injuries and, safer working conditions. It took years with terrible sacrifices by many men to get these changes made.

The miners were also harassed by hired thugs who were paid by the mining companies and even by their own government, which called out the National Guard to quell the unrest. One of the things that made America great was the final compromise, which was the result of management and labor realizing that they had to have each other. Another benefit of the conflict was that any inexperienced prospect for employment was required to take a comprehensive course in safety. This course covered all potential dangers and taught the beginning miner how to deal with them.

Even with improved working conditions, accidents happen in all walks of life and mining is no exception. On May 2, 1972, probably as a result of spontaneous combustion, a fire started in old rotting timbers and other refuse, which might have been smoldering for some time, before it finally burned through sealed off bulkheads. When that happened, the deadly carbon monoxide gases were released into the mine's air supply. Ninety one men of the 173 men working at the time died of suffocation.

The fire continued for five months, consuming timbers and refuse that might have yielded some evidence as to the cause of the fire. Most of the area where the fire first started had caved in. The refuse was paper, rags, empty oil containers and explosives cartons which had been stacked throughout the mine near scrap timbers. Even though the area at the 3400 to 3550 levels had been sealed off, leaking air probably kept the temperature at about that of spontaneous combustion. It was felt that no one person who was at the mine on the day of the fire was in charge, since most of the executives and top level personnel were attending a stockholder's meeting.

Dozens of lawsuits were filed against the Sunshine Mining Company, by lawyers, who were representing the wives and families of the men killed. This was understandable as these families had suffered great losses.

The miners had spent many, long, cold mornings standing in line, of their own free will desperately hoping that they would get a job, working at the only trade that they knew. I cannot believe any of them would have hired a lawyer after the disastrous fire, to file a lawsuit, any more than they would have, if a rock had fallen on their head. If the dead could talk, I believe they would have said, "Lawsuit! What the hell for? I knew the dangers of my job, when I chose this way to make a living." I know that after working underground for some time I was as comfortable and confident as any other job I had ever done.

Between Wallace and Kellogg, Idaho a memorial was built in remembrance of these men. It stands as a tribute to all the good men who do their life's work in mining.

Mining Memorial

Sometimes happenings prove the old adage, "What goes around comes around." Our grandson Jim met a girl from Mullan, Idaho, while in college at Boise State University. Her name is Wendy. Her grandfather and her father had spent their lives working in the mines. Her father still works there and is a shift boss in one of the mines.

When they were married the reception was put on by the town itself, for one of their own. The flowers and food could not have been duplicated anywhere in the world. I sat there watching these strong, hard working people, who had lived through depressions, lay-offs, and labor strikes, but still tried to provide a better life for their children. Both Wendy and her sister are college graduates. Places such as this are the true example of America's greatness.

I had worked in the mine all winter, and now that spring was so close, I decided to make my way back to the Boise Valley. I took a different road home this time and ended up going through a town called Hermiston, Oregon. I stopped to get gas and something to eat and while having a beer, I started to talk to a guy who was working for a construction company that had a cost-plus contract to build igloos. I said, "Why in the hell do they need igloos? There is not an Eskimo within five thousand miles." At this he looked at me strangely, saw that I was serious and started laughing so hard he almost fell off the bar stool. I began to get a little upset, so he quickly explained that these igloos were long concrete buildings, shaped like an igloo, but built with thick concrete reinforced roofs covered with dirt to be used to store bombs, shells and other types of military ordinance. As this was a cost-plus job the company was hiring men, paying good wages and evidently the more money they spent, the more they made.

An Igloo

Almost 7000 men were working eight hour shifts day and night. The smaller igloos were 61 feet long and 24 feet wide. The longer ones were 80 x 30 feet. These large bunkers used about 375 yards of concrete. The sides and ends were 10 inches thick with reinforced concrete. The top was only half as thick, so that in case of an explosion, the blast would be directed upward. The doors were like bank vault doors and wide enough to drive a truck through. The entire igloo was covered with sand. There was no shortage of fine sand and the constant wind drove it through every crack and filled every crevice of the surroundings.

The job sounded good to me and my bar friend steered me to the right place where I easily got a job. It was good to be out in the sun again. I found a nice place to set up my tent, bought some groceries and was home. It looked so good I got a post office box, wrote Lorraine a letter telling her where I was and that I didn't know when I'd see her. In a few days she wrote me saying how disappointed she was that I wasn't coming home. She went on to say, for the first time in our association, how much she liked me and how much she missed me.

What was wrong with that girl? I had nothing to offer and her letter put me in a private hell; wishing it could be, yet thinking it would never work. I felt in all fairness that it was time to tell her this, so I bought her a beautiful rose gold wrist watch, wrote quite an emotional letter trying to explain that my prospects were not too great; and that this was my farewell gift. I mailed the watch along with my master piece of a letter, quit my job the next day and almost got to her house before the watch and letter arrived. So much for being noble!

It was the summer of 1941 and I was twenty three years old. While driving down the highway, I started thinking that maybe, just maybe, I could amount to something. Even though I was not educated like Lorraine and her family, I was not stupid, was a damn good man, and could earn good money. I thought if this untouchable girl would have me, why couldn't I dream about our having a happy life together? With this thought uppermost in my mind, as soon as I got to Boise, I rented a room, got cleaned up and with a lot of hope, gave her a call.

She was very glad to hear my voice and loved her new watch. She said that my profound letter was ridiculous and wanted to see me as soon as possible. She is a nineteen year old sophomore at the college in Caldwell, Idaho living in a small apartment with her sister, Mary. She gave me directions to her apartment and wanted me to come and get her. Could I finally hope that I am not dreaming and that someone cares for me just as I am. I felt a delicious excitement just thinking about it.

We dated, and finally talked about getting married; how many children we wanted, a daughter first to help out, then three boys. I had gone to work at Anderson Ranch dam on the south fork of the Boise River, working in a shaft about eight feet square that was being sunk below the river bed. The shaft was to be drilled some hundred feet straight down and was exceedingly dangerous work. Holes were drilled in the bottom of this shaft using a ninety pound jack hammer, and then they were loaded with dynamite. Due to the amount of water leaking through the walls, it was necessary to thoroughly tar the fuses to waterproof them. The only way to remove the blasted rock was to load it into a large steel bucket attached to a cable coming from a hoist drum on the surface. This steel bucket was about three feet in diameter and four feet long. This was also the way you got up and down the shaft. So when you lit the fuses and signaled the hoist man to bring you up, you hoped to hell that he had not gone to sleep.

Once the shaft was completed, a horizontal tunnel was drilled under the river in order to pour the concrete core that would be the base for an earth filled dam, supposedly one of the highest in the country. After a couple of months of doing this I was asked to be tunnel foreman on the graveyard shift. I was twenty three years old and found myself supervising eight or ten men of all ages. My first night was New Year's Eve and I suggested that we all sit down, and have a smoke, so that we wouldn't start the new year working for a living. This was appreciated by the men and made my job easier, as the things I didn't know, they were willing to help me learn.

The tunnel was approximately 24 feet in diameter with 8 or 10 automatic air hammers mounted on a large structure, called a Jumbo. This Jumbo had wheels like a train and was moved forward on it's tracks to where holes were to be drilled to blast out the rock. After a blast the Jumbo was moved out of the way and a huge mucking machine would place the blasted rock onto a conveyor belt, from which it was dumped into large Euclid trucks that hauled it out of the tunnel. Tracks were added and the Jumbo was moved ahead and the whole process was repeated until the tunnel was finished.

When the tunnel was finished, I became the batch plant foreman and mixed the concrete used to line the twenty four foot diameter tunnel walls. The batch plant had three large hoppers or bins some twenty feet off the ground. These were filled, one with sand, one with three quarter inch rock and the other with cement. From these, using a large scale, the proper amount of rock, sand and cement was weighed, and dumped into the large mixers. Water was added to make the proper consistency of the concrete, which was very important. A cone shaped measuring device was used to provide a slump test to guarantee its consistency. A track ran under the chute and concrete filled torpedo-shaped cars that hauled the concrete into the tunnel, where it was pumped behind a steel form and left to set up. After it was set up, the form was collapsed slightly and moved on tracks to the next pour. I was making good money at the dam. In fact, one Sunday, I had worked my regular day shift from eight a.m. to four thirty p.m. The swing shift operator who was supposed to replace me from four thirty p.m. to midnight did not show up, so it was necessary for me to work his shift also. This was a sixteen hour day and a Sunday, so I was paid double time wages.

Lorraine and I picked out a diamond engagement and wedding ring and announced our intention to get married. Because of her father's illness, her brother Louis had, to some extent, assumed the role as head of the family.

He was quite emphatic in his objections to Lorraine's announcement, and was seconded by her sister Mary. Since Lorraine's father was ill, I didn't get any serious objection from him. It didn't seem to impress anyone that I made more money in two weeks than the president of the college made in a month. Of course, it was quite obvious that he was using his mind instead of his back. It finally got to the point that Lorraine told her brother and sister that if they didn't accept our decision, that they wouldn't be invited to the wedding. What a gal! Lorraine and I had wholeheartedly agreed that she was to finish her education; and now I would be in a position to make this a lot easier for her financially. In turn, I believed that I had been educated in a tough school of hard knocks, and felt that I could meet any person or obstacle head on and end up the survivor.

Pearl harbor was bombed December 7, 1941. All the eligible young men and women joined the service. I was still working at Anderson Dam, had no intention of rushing off to get shot at. But we knew I probably would not escape the draft, so because of this we, set January 25, 1942 as our wedding date. Many of the men that I had worked with were going to Guam or Wake Island. Most of them were either killed or tortured by the Japanese. For some reason Lorraine never thought it was very funny when I would say that it was a tough decision for me to make: being killed, tortured or getting married.

We were married in a small Christian church in the town close to where her family lived and not far from the Jackson's farm. Lorraine wore her mother's wedding dress and veil and was absolutely beautiful. I wore my new suit and we made a fine looking couple. The church was packed with well wishers, who knew my background and Lorraine's family and were delighted that we would be given a chance for happiness. When the minister

asked the question, "Do you take this woman to be your lawfully wedded wife, to love, honor, and obey till death do you part?", there will never be a response of "I do" spoken with more promise than mine.

We had made reservations at the Hotel Utah in Salt Lake City for our honeymoon and were to fly there from Boise. The family and many friends went out to the airport with us where we boarded a two engine plane. Flying was not too common then and I'm sure some felt that they were waving good bye for the last time. I almost felt the same way. I hadn't minded dropping four or five thousand feet into the mines but going up in an airplane was different. That first step was a doozy.

We arrived safely, took a cab to the hotel, and were shown to a really nice room. Even with my experience in sex, I didn't know what to do. I knew Lorraine was innocent in this area, so suggested we go get something to eat. The hotel had a nice restaurant and in our nervousness we ordered a celebration dinner, then sat picking at this fine meal and finally gave up and went back to our room. We were both tired from the long day of excitement. Lorraine was at a complete loss. We finally took off our clothes. I held that beautiful body in my arms and actually cried from wonder and happiness, then we both went sound asleep.

It was good thing that we had rested. Lorraine had helped take care of three younger brothers and certainly knew what a male body looked like. But I know she had never seen anything like what I displayed. We had agreed to wait on children until the threat of war was settled, so I had the proper prevention for pregnancy. I was slow and gentle and after the first time she began to enjoy the act. We hung a "Do not disturb" sign on the door and finally went to eat late that evening. We had four days of bliss, then we took the train back to Boise. We had a Pullman car and even though I had ridden many miles in a freight car listening to the clickity clack of the wheels, I will never forget that ride home with my bride.

Lorraine went back to school and I went back to my job at the dam. We spent weekends together and when her school got out in the spring I had found us a small cabin next to the river above the dam construction site. We set up housekeeping and I counted the hours until it was time to quit and hurry home. Then we decided that we wanted to start our family. If I were drafted and didn't make it back, Lorraine would have a part of me. If I did come back I would have a family.

The job at the dam was almost finished and we decided to go to Pocatello, Idaho where an airfield was being built. I got a job running a huge rock crusher. We had a nice apartment with no worries, except the escalating war. Due to the frantic war effort, I was making unheard of wages. I would cash my pay check, throw the money over the bed and we would make love. Later on, as the children grew up, and each of them became successful in their chosen fields, I have no doubt that making love on a layer of twenty dollar bills imprinted on them a desire for monetary rewards.

I had heard that the Sea Bees were taking construction men, and that in some cases they were going in with an officer's commission. I figured that if anyone would qualify for a commission, I could, as I had run heavy equipment, knew dynamite, had supervised men and should be what they wanted. Unfortunately I never found out. I sat in their recruitment office for over three hours while they talked to fresh faced kids not dry behind the ears yet and finally I said, "The hell with it", thinking, " I don't have to stand in line to join anything." Was I ever proven wrong. I did get drafted and had to be in Boise in October to be inducted. I passed the physical and was to go with forty or fifty other inducted men to Fort Douglas, Utah for assignment. After taking written tests we were informed that since our overall scores were so high we were to be put in the Air Corps. In our bunch were three young Indian boys from the Fort Hall Indian reservation. In looking at them and at the rest of us I thought they were probably the ones who had brought our scores up.

Lorraine had said goodbye, cried a little, and went back to live with her folks. Her mother persuaded her to return to college. We had bought a new 1941 Chevrolet five passenger coupe which she was proud of and I knew she would be well taken care of by her family. We recruits were sent to St. Petersburg, Florida to take basic training. Now, going back to when I said I was wrong about standing in lines, we stood in lines for everything! We learned to march up and down the sandy beaches, and the humidity almost did us mountain boys in. You could wash a pair of socks, hang them out to dry and they would stay wet. My three Indian friends couldn't seem to learn the left right, left right drill so the drill sergeant finally told them to go sit in the shade of a tree out of the way. We smart S.O.B.s are still marching up and down in the hot sun. I was more convinced than ever that they were the ones who brought our entry scores up. I often wondered what happened to them. I would not be surprised if they didn't end up being Generals. I regretted many times not waiting longer to join the Sea Bees, especially when some little pip squeak with a P.F.C. stripe barked orders or personally ridiculed you, if a mistake was made.

Lorraine was pregnant and we decided that if our baby was a girl, we would name her Kay Lorraine. Kay was born on December 29, 1942. I wish I had been there, but like thousands of other soldiers who became fathers I would have to wait. The main thing was that both were doing O.K. Basic training was finished and some of us were being sent to Buckley Field at Denver, Colorado to armament school. This was to teach us to assemble and repair all types of weapons, especially the fifty caliber machine guns. While there they requested that any of us wanting to go to gunnery school should sign up. I signed up and was on my back to Tyndall Field in Florida. We spent days shooting shotguns, instead of machine guns, to teach us how to lead a moving target. Then we flew in the rear seat of a plane, shooting a thirty caliber machine gun at tow targets, pulled by another plane. All in all, it was fun. From Florida we were sent to Salt Lake City to heavy bombardment school, learning about all types of bombs. One day we were notified that we would soon be assigned to an airfield for actual training in bombers.

It looked like most of us would be sent to Clovis Field in New Mexico, but there was also a rumor that Gowen Field in Boise, Idaho was a possibility. You had to get permission to even speak to a commanding officer, which I managed to do, and requested that I be sent to Gowen Field, as I had a baby daughter close by whom I hadn't yet seen. He seemed like a decent person but pointed out that it was against military policy to allow soldiers to be near their homes. I had to accept this, yet was saddened by the possibility of being so close yet not seeing Lorraine and my daughter.

Some three thousand of us stood on the railway platform waiting to board the troop trains. Hours went by as soldiers filled the many cars. Finally only about forty of us were left. We wondered what was wrong when a passenger train pulled in and we were loaded in a car. It pulled out and was headed north and the word was that we were going to Gowen Field. I wished that I could have thanked the officer who allowed this assignment to happen It took most of the day, and after we reached southern Idaho I spent most of the time looking out the train window, with eager anticipation. Many ribald comments were being made about what a desolate God forsaken country it was; but I loved every sage brush and pile of lava rock we passed. When we arrived at Gowen Field they said we had to stay on the base overnight to get settled in, but would be issued a pass the next day to see the town.

I had already written Lorraine telling her I was probably going to be sent to Clovis Field in New Mexico, so when I called her, she assumed that was where I was. It took some convincing before she could believe that I was actually in Idaho; but she finally became overjoyed and was to pick me up at the gate the next day. We had a tearful reunion at the gate, Lorraine and I and my daughter. She was about seven months old, didn't know me and wasn't too happy when I tried to hold her. It was nice to know that I finally belonged to a family!

I was assigned as a waist gunner on a B-24 bomber and had to be at the base most of the time. Still the three of us spent lots of time together. We finished our first phase training at Gowen Field and were to go to Scottsbluff, Nebraska for second phase training. Lorraine was to go back to college so the day came when we had to say good bye again. I was glad to meet my daughter and if it was to be the last time at least I knew what she looked like. At Scottsbluff we continued training with mock bombing runs. The bombardiers were learning to use the Norden bomb sight. There were ten men on a B-24, the pilot, co-pilot, navigator and bombardier, all officers. The rest of us were enlisted men, a radio operator, ball turret gunner, nose turret gunner, top turret gunner, tail gunner and a waist gunner, me. Along with being a waist gunner, another one of my duties was to walk along a narrow cat-walk in the bomb bay to release the safety pins on the bombs. The bombs were equipped with a small propeller on their noses, which prevented them from exploding before we reached the target. At the time the bombs were to be released to hit a target this safety pin had to be removed so that the propeller would spin off the bomb, exposing a plunger that exploded the bombs on impact.

All towns had a U.S.O. with dances and other entertainment to keep the younger boys from getting too home sick. Our tail gunner was a little Irish boy named Jimmy O'Brian. He met a local home-town girl at one of the USO dances. They dated, fell in love and wrote to each other until we finally finished our missions and returned home. They had made their promises to each other by V mail, so he headed for Scottsbluff to get married. They live in Arizona now, have raised four children and have been married for all these years.

From Scottsbluff we went to Langley Field, Virginia for our final third phase training and from there we would be headed for overseas. Lorraine's brother, Louis had gotten a scholarship to medical school in Chicago; and when we learned we were to pick up a new B-24 at Mitchel Field in New York, he agreed to meet Lorraine and Kay in Chicago, and help her get to New York, so that we could have some time together. Brave girl that she was, she packed two suitcases of diapers and clothes, got on a train which was full of soldiers and made the trip.

Even though the soldiers carried her suitcases, made a place for her to sit and sometimes held Kay it was a long trip. Louis met her and they came to New York. I had arranged for a room in the Garden City Hotel on Long Island. However, at Mitchell Field I was restricted to the base for security reasons, but I slipped out each day so that we could be together. Kay was almost a year old, so we got acquainted. I told Lorraine that when she heard the planes taking off, it would be time for her to go home. Only four days later, the day before Christmas, we took off, with me looking down at the hotel, and I was sure, with her looking up. I couldn't help wondering why I was doing this. It was not for God or country, nor was I mad enough at anybody enough to want to kill them. I was leaving my girl and baby behind me and heading off toward the unknown. I could only think that I had never been a quitter and since I had gotten into this mess I must see it through. How sad, I felt.

This poem reflects my feelings at this time.

I asked a friend whom I knew to be a veteran what Veteran's Day meant to him. And I listened carefully to what he had to say:

"I don't know quite where to begin", he said slowly,

    "for me, the meaning is mostly in my heart."

"I am proud to be an American who responded to his country's call,

and when called upon, I did my part.

Did I fight for your freedom? Yes! Our politicians will tell you,

    as they strut and pontificate this Veteran's Day.

Flags and red, white and blue bunting will adorn their platforms,

    as they glamorize sending young Americans into harm's way."

"Did I fight for your freedom? It's very difficult to say.

    I have to remind you of a sign that adorns a place nearby.

Placed prominently on the green of the Boise Veterans Hospital.

    In bold letters that have made some cry.

It says in patriotic language so noble and so American,

    "THE PRICE OF FREEDOM IS VISABLE HERE"

But many of the veterans who visit there will be reluctant to tell you

    Only if you have been in combat, is that message really clear."

"Did I fight for your freedom? Hell no! is my first response.

    I fought for the lives of friends and comrades caught in dark places.

Under fire, and besieged with stress unknown to most,

    killing other men and never quite able to forget they had faces.

Unable to have the luxury of grief for good friends suddenly dead,

    your particular freedom nor anyone else's ever crossed my mind.

At least not then, and would not even now as I ponder these thoughts,

    except, somehow reason has to be found for those left behind."

"Did I fight for your freedom? I guess I did, and for mine too.

    Some understanding person, maybe who even had been there,

realized Veterans needed their day, a day of parades, remembrances,

    small American flags on Veteran graves, help for the cross we bear

Freedom, the word is over used, maybe appropriate for Veteran's Day,

    gives a tangible reason why wars must be fought.

Do not forget, as sweet as the word freedom sounds and is over used,

    freedom as you know it, was very dearly bought."

Last night they came to see me in my deep sleep, still young while I am old.

    Sweede, Mel, others, whispering approval of what I just told.

Printed with permission from: K.W. Andy Andrus

                                                             Colonel USMC Ret

It was an adventure though and I suppose this is why there will always be
wars with young men seeing only the glamour, thinking they are invulner-
able and someone else will catch the bullet or have an arm or leg blown off.
You would think that we could learn, but man never has; and since the
beginning of time, we have continued to kill each other. One dubious
benefit of war is that it is the best form of birth control known to the
world, when you consider the millions of young men who have been killed.

We flew to Trinidad and stayed there for a couple of days for gas and a
maintenance check on the new plane. I was introduced to fresh pineapple
which I had never eaten before in my life, and got such a case of gut ache,
and diarrhea that I would just as soon have been shot now as waiting till
later. From Trinidad we flew to Belem on the east coast of South America,
over miles of jungle and the great Amazon River. At Belem we stayed for a
couple of weeks so that belly tanks could be installed in the bomb bays in
order to have enough gas to get across the ocean to Africa. It was a jungle
city with some industry, but mainly natives who flocked in from all over
the country because of the military base and the rich American soldiers. If
you had ever sat through an army film showing the results of venereal
disease, it would be almost enough to make you give up sex altogether. But
the young guys went wild, throwing all caution to the wind, and many
ended up being treated for whatever disease they caught. In my case I
could never have violated the trust that I knew Lorraine and I had in each
other.

The tanks were finally installed and each plane took off across the ocean
toward Dakar on the west coast of Africa. It was about a twelve hour flight
and after seeing nothing but water, hoping the navigator knew where we
were and that the engines wouldn't quit, it was good to see the coast. We
landed at Dakar, fueled the plane and went to Americats, then to northern
Africa just below Tunis. Our destination was called Cape Bond and the
Germans had recently retreated from there to Italy. We stayed there for over
a month living in tents. There were acres of fuel dumps, and every German

vehicle made, from motorcycles staff cars, to tanks, and trucks and most were in running condition. The mess hall and cook tents were a quarter mile or so from our tents and at meal time there would be a long line of these vehicles which we drove just to eat. We made stoves by cutting fifty five gallon barrels in half, set another barrel outside which was full of gas, and used eighty millimeter shell casings for chimneys. Copper tubing from the gas barrel dripped gas into our stove and provided good heat. The Italian soldiers had suffered terrible losses because of the absolute single minded direction of Mussolini who had over-ruled any input by his commanders. Their situation finally became hopeless and they surrendered to the Allies. Such hate was felt toward the "Duce", that a group of volunteers shot him and his mistress, then hung them by their heels from the girders of a Milan service station. After hanging ignominiously for a day, the allies cut them down. So ended another dictator, Benito Mussolini, "Il Duce", premier of Italy from 1922 to 1943.

We were then to fly to a place called San Gioranni, which had been a monastery close to a town called Cerignola, Italy. The first plane was loaded with our stoves, and a couple of motorcycles, and was so heavy it couldn't get in the air. It crashed and burned and most of its crew was lost, so the whole operation was stopped and we had to unload all of our loot.

Runways and a tent city with all facilities had been built at Cerignola, waiting for our arrival. The fun and games were over and we all had degrees of concern as we were faced with our first mission, realizing that the odds were that we would be killed. This was pointed out plainly at our first briefing when they informed us that we had no long range fighter planes to escort us past a certain distance. Most of the targets were beyond this limit and from this it was obvious that we were expendable. However, we were not helpless, as each plane carried twelve fifty caliber machine guns and due to our training could lay down a wall of lead that was quite accurate. This was the fifteenth Air Force 455th bomb group with four squadrons, the 741, 742, 743 and 744. I was in the 743.

I am in the back row, third from the left.

Our first plane was named Menacing Messilena and on our eighth mission was shot up so badly that we were forced to fall behind formation on the way back. This was when a plane was the most vulnerable as German fighter planes would delight in playing cat and mouse and finally shooting it down. We spent anxious minutes watching for any sign of them coming; and it was not long before the top turret gunner reported two planes rapidly overtaking us from behind.

We were resigned to our fate and determined to fight, when he identified the two planes as P-51's, which were mustang fighters and some of the best fighters produced by the United States. As they dropped in beside us, we could see that these planes were flown by members of the Tuskegee Airmen, an all black squadron of fighter pilots. They stayed with us escorting us, to safety. We couldn't stay in the air long enough to get to our home base and had to land on a fighter field close to Rome. Poor old Menacing Messilena ended up a Menacing Mess and was so badly damaged it couldn't be salvaged; but we all walked away without a scratch.

Menacing Messilena

We were taken into Rome, put up in a nice hotel and were told that a truck would come from our base to get us in a couple of days. All of us carried a survival packet, compass, etc., in case we were forced to bail out and maybe work our way back to the base. In this packet was fifty dollars to use as bribes. We put this to good use, bribing drinks, good meals, entertainment, taxis and touring this famous old city. The fifth army had spent the winter in pup tents up in the mountains and many of the G.I.s were in town for R & R (Rest and Relaxation). They were a bearded, mean bunch, had trench knives on their belts and hated the Air Force. They had watched us fly over their fox holes, while eating their K rations, and thought we lived in luxury. It didn't help to see us with wings on our chest and wearing our crushed caps. Discretion told us that when they came down the sidewalk we stepped out of their way. Once four or five of them were asked to go on a mission with us. It happened to be a rough one with lots of anti-aircraft flak, German fighter planes, bombers either shot down by enemy fighters or hit by flak. I think they prayed to get back in their foxhole.

Tepee Time Gal

We got back to our base and were given a brand new plane. Someone came up with the name Tepee Time Gal, and an Italian artist painted a beautiful Indian girl about six feet tall, well stacked, wearing a long red dress. We thought she looked sexy and so did the German fighter pilots. I swear they made extra passes at us just to see her. They finally put droppable wing tanks for gas on P 51's, and now we had fighter escort all the way into our targets and back. It was the early part of the war and we flew almost every day if the weather was good. The main targets were marshaling railroad yards, oil fields, ball bearing factories and any thing else that, if hit, would cripple the German war machine. When the army hit the Anzio beach head, we made a low bombing run dropping five hundred pound bombs ahead of the invasion. Word came back that many of the defenders were wiped out and several hundred others were stunned and wandering around in a daze from the concussions.

We were required to fly fifty missions. Some were not too tough and were counted as one mission but most of them were terrible, with heavy losses, and these would be counted as two. The Germans had developed a type of radar that could lock onto a bomber's altitude and path of flight. It was our tail gunner's job to watch for these bursts of flak and if they were headed our way to tell the pilot to move the hell over. This problem was solved, when it was learned that by throwing out strips of aluminum foil, it effectively confused the radar.

We went over the Polesti oil fields two times, and each time the flak was so heavy that it looked like you could walk on it. After each bombing run the German fighter planes would attach us like a swarm of angry bees. We got hit by fragments of flak many times, yet never suffered any serious damage. The black smoke could be seen from the burning oil fires for many miles. The planes, which were hit over the target and forcing the crew to bail out, were in the middle of the smoke. The crew members parachuting out died from suffocation.

You can see a white square patch at the bottom right-hand corner of my window in the picture (next page). A piece of flak came through the thin skin of the plane headed for my stomach, but was deflected by a metal strut and went up through the roof. I have always denied divine intervention in any part of our existence, but I seem to remember saying, "Hey, thanks Old Man!"

None of our crew got hit. Our most terrifying experience was when we were flying at some twenty thousand feet and all four super chargers quit. A supercharger simply provided more air to the engines and when they quit the plane immediately started down. A B-24 had a glide angle of about a thousand feet a minute which is quite steep. During this decent the bombardier's ears were hurting so badly from the change in pressure, that he was yelling, "level out, level out". It sounded over the intercom like "bail out!, bail out!" but because the plane was dropping so fast, you were suspended in air and were helpless to move. Ten minutes can seem like forever, but around ten thousand feet the engines began to get enough oxygen to run, and we barely managed to level out. I was no stranger to death having worked in places where men had been killed; so could handle this terrifying time better than some of the others. All the other men were younger than I; and I was affectionately called "Pop". The radio operator was also the waist gunner opposite my side and he had curled up in a fetal position crying hysterically. I cradled him in my arms, rocked him back and forth, talking quietly until he took some deep breaths and settled down. He was just a kid; and I convinced him that anyone who said they weren't scared was a liar, including me. He was ashamed about the way he had acted; but I told him no one would ever know. We finished our fifty missions, picked up several more flak holes, and managed to shoot down a couple of German fighter planes. Finally we were eligible to return home.

Our group received two unit citations and the air medal with five oak leaf clusters.

The following is a list of the missions our crew flew:

Soldier participated in the following Bombing Missions, targets, diversionary flights and patrols:

1944	Feb 25 - *Graz, Austria	"	12 -	La Spezia, Italy
	Mar 3 - Fabrica Di Roma, Italy	"	14 -	Piacenza, San Damiano
	" 17 - *Vienna, Austria	"	18 -	*Ploesti, Rumania
	" 19 - Graz, Austria	"	22 -	La Spezia, Italy
	" 22 - Bologna, Italy	"	23 -	Nemi, Italy (Rome Area)
	" 24 - Rimini, Italy	"	24 -	*Vienna, Austria
	Apr 3 - *Budapest, Hunstanard	"	26 -	Grenoble, France
	" 4 - *Bucharest, Rumania	"	27 -	Montepellier, France
	" 7 - Bologna, Italy	"	28 -	Genoa, Italy
	" 12 - *Bad Voslau, Austria	"	29 -	Bos Krupa, Yugoslavia
	" 20 - Monfalcone, Italy	"	29 -	Banja Luka, Yugoslavia
	" 23 - *Bad Voslau, Austria	"	30 -	*Wels, Austria
	" 24 - *Bucharest, Rumania	Jun	4 -	Genoa, Italy
	Apr 25 - Turin, Italy	"	6 -	*Brasov, Rumania
	" 30 - Milan, Italy	"	10 -	Ferrara, Italy
	May 5 - *Ploesti, Rumania	"	11 -	*Giurgui, Rumania
	" 6 - *Campina, Rumania	"	16 -	*Vienna, Austria
	" 10 - *Wiener, Neustadt, Austria	"	26 -	*Moosbierbaum, Austria

(*Double Sorti Credit) A Double Sorti Credit is an exceptionally dangerous mission and was counted as two missions.

RESTRICTED

HEADQUARTERS
FIFTEENTH AIR FORCE
APO   520

GENERAL ORDERS   15 January 1945
NUMBER 232

Citation of Unit - - - - - - - - - - - - - - - - - - - - - - - - - - - - - - - Section I
SECTION I - <u>CITATION OF UNIT</u>

      Under the provisions of Circular No. 333, War Department, 1943 and Circular No. 89, Headquarters NATOUSA. 10 July 1944, the following unit is cited for outstanding performance of duty in armed conflict with the enemy.

      <u>455th BOMBARDMENT GROUP.</u> For outstanding performance of duty in armed conflict with the enemy. Notified to prepare maximum aircraft for a mission against the highly important and heavily defended Moosbierbaum Oil Refinery, Moosbierbaum, Austria, the ground crews, despite acute shortages in personnel and equipment, worked untiringly and with grim determination to have their aircraft in the peak of mechanical condition to insure the success of this vital operation. On 26 June 1944, thirty-six (36) B-24 type aircraft, heavily loaded with maximum tonnage, were airborne, and assuming the lead of the other groups of their Wing, set course for their destination. In-route to the target the formation was intercepted by approximately twenty (20) twin-engine enemy fighters which were engaged by the escorting fighters. Immediately thereafter, the bomber formation was attacked by approximately sixty (60) additional twin-engine fighters in a series of vicious head-on attacks, firing rockets, heavy machine guns and 20mm cannon in a desperate effort to destroy the bomber formation. Nearing the target sixty (60) more single engine fighters joined in the aggressive and relentless attacks against the Group's formation. Heedless of this seemingly overwhelming opposition, the gallant crew members battled their way through the heavy enemy fire to the objective. One of the bombers, after colliding with an attacking fighter, remained persistently with the formation for the bombing run before dropping out in flames. Two other bombers set on fire by enemy gun fire, continued over the target, successfully dropped their bombs and then exploded in mid-air. With complete disregard for the continued heavy opposition, displaying outstanding courage, leadership and fortitude, the Group held its lead of the Wing

formation, bringing it through the enemy defenses for a highly successful bombing run. The oil storage area of the refinery was heavily hit with large fires started. Eight direct hits were sustained by the power station and numerous rolling stock and vital installations were severely damaged throughout the plant area. During the fierce aerial battle to the target, the gallant gunners of the Group, through their skill and determination in the defense of their formation, accounted for thirty-four (34) enemy fighters destroyed, to hold the losses of their Group to ten (10) heavy bombers. By the conspicuous gallantry, professional skill and determination of the combat crews, together with the superior technical skill and devotion to duty of the ground personnel, the 455th Bombardment Group had upheld the highest tradition of the Military Service, thereby reflecting great credit upon itself and the Armed Forces of the United States of America

BY COMMAND OF MAJOR GENERAL TWINING.

> R.K. Taylor,
> Colonel, GSC,
> Chief of Staff

OFFICIAL:
> /s/ J.M. Ivins
> /s/ J.M. Ivins
> Colonel, AGD,
> Adjutant General

RESTRICTED

This is to certify that in accordance with General Order Number 232, Headquarters, Fifteenth Air Force, dated 15 January 1945, the following named individual was a member of the 455th Bombardment Group (Heavy) on 26 June 1944, and, in accordance with AR 600-45, as amended, is entitled to wear the War Department Distinguished Unit Citation Badge and/or the First Oak Leaf Cluster to the War Department Distinguished Unit Citation Badge in accordance with existing regulations pertaining to same.

TECHNICAL SERGEANT: HOSAC, CHESTER W.   39902561

During World War II, when a family member was killed, the family was notified by telegram. The telegram became the most dreaded of events. Unknowingly, I sent Lorraine a telegram which scared everyone until she opened it and read the good news that I was coming home. After each mission we were issued a good shot of whisky. We knew that we would be sent to the Isle of Capri for rest and relaxation, so we had saved up our ration of whiskey plus that of those who didn't drink and we had a good supply of whiskey along with wine, which was plentiful. The Air Force had taken over the hotels on the island so we lived in the lap of luxury, went through the Blue Grotto, got drunk and finally received word to return to Rome to board a ship for home. It was a liberty ship and was crammed with returning airmen. The food was terrible and you tasted it twice, once going down and then when it came back up. Half of the trip was spent throwing up. We finally got to Newport News, Virginia and were met with a band which made us feel like heroes. We were escorted to a mess hall and fed a sumptuous meal. Ten gallon cans of cold milk were set down the aisles and not having had any milk during my time overseas, it was unbelievably good.

We were put on a passenger train with banners on the side saying 455th bomb group. We were still drinking some. The conductor was an ex-marine and we twisted his arm into having a drink with us and sang "Off we go into the wild blue yonder". Our ex-marine got loaded. We put his conductors cap and coat on one of our guys who then collected tickets from everyone. It is doubtful it was ever straightened out. We arrived back at Fort Douglas, Utah the worse for wear and were processed, given a ticket home and a thirty day delay in route, and were to report to Santa Monica, California. Lorraine and Kay met me at the bus station in Boise where we had a tearful reunion. Lorraine and I were crying, with Kay crying the loudest because her mother was crying, and hugging some strange man.

We had our Chevy coupe that by now was a real prize as no new cars had been made during the war. We had a flat tire before getting to Nampa, and I could see that all the tires were worn. Civilians couldn't buy tires but being a returning veteran I could get a permit to buy new tires. We rented a motel room, stayed in Nampa for a few days, visiting her folks and friends, then took off up through Oregon, and Washington and down the west coast to Santa Monica, California

I had to be processed for redistribution, part of which included being interviewed by a psychiatrist who wanted to know if I had suffered any trauma from combat. I assured him I had, having had the crap scared out of me, while wearing a flying suit at fifty degrees below zero. Asking me if I ever slept with my mother, I could answer that one truthfully, as I was never around her. I did point out though that I had slept with my wife, and had a baby to prove it. He was far crazier than I was, but dutifully put it all down and declared me sane and still fit. I found out later that had I not been such a damn smart ass, I could have been sent to a luxury rehabilitation center in Spokane, Washington. Instead I was given the choice of going over seas for another tour of duty or entering the cadet program at San Antonio, Texas. I chose the latter.

I had to report to a place called Eagle Pass, Texas while waiting to enter the cadet program so I sent Lorraine and Kay in the car to Fort Worth, Texas where Lorraine had been born, and she was to stay with her cousin and husband. Twelve of us were sent to Eagle Pass, Texas on a troop train, which was a training field for pilots. We were the first combat veterans to be assigned there and the commanding officer had us come to his office so he could listen to our stories about the war. We were eligible for flight pay which was one half more than our base pay. I got acquainted with a gung-ho youngster, talked him into going on flights, then signed my name to get this extra money.

Finally I was sent to San Antonio, Texas and entered a ten week cadet program. I called Lorraine and she had found us a room. Even though I was restricted to base, I managed to be along the road where she picked me up most nights. I stuck out the ten weeks, and learned Morse Code. I never understood why we had to learn Morse Code, as there was no possible place where we could use it. I'm not sure of this, but I think "…—…" meant S.O.S., which was a universal distress signal. I guess if I had ever gotten lost, while hunting elk, I could send up smoke signals using Morse Code. We also learned to identify enemy aircraft, most of which had been trying to kill me just a few months back. After the ten weeks I resigned the Cadet program, and as the war was winding down, I didn't have to go back overseas.

We were then sent to San Angelo, Texas to another base where we found a small apartment and I checked into the base by midnight. The next morning, while still asleep, I was shaken awake and there stood my bombardier from all my missions. He had ended up a squadron commander, so he got me a cushy job checking vaccine shots supposedly;　gave me a class A pass and since we had the Chevy car, and he didn't have a car we could drive out to the base together. We spent many pleasant days with him and his wife. Our first son, Steve was born in the hospital at San Angelo. Two babies were born that night Steve and a girl. Years later when Steve was in junior high school in Boise, a new girl was introduced to the class. The teacher said she had been born in San Angelo, Texas. Steve told her he also was born in San Angelo. She said, "Yeah sure" but it was the same girl. What a coincidence that was, considering all the thousands of G.I. babies who were born all over the world.

CHAPTER 9
A DREAM IS FULFILLED

The armed services had a point system and if you had enough points you were eligible for discharge. My bombardier assured me a field commission if I wanted to stay in, but there was no way I could put up with all that regimentation, so we stacked the back seat of our car with clothes and bedding, to make it level with the front seat for Kay and the baby, and headed for Idaho.

The service had taken two years and ten months out of my life and as we drove the long road home, I spent a lot of time thinking about this period of time. I still didn't believe in God or Divine Intervention in the scheme of things, and often had wondered, when the Chaplain prayed for us before a mission during which we dropped five hundred pound bombs undoubtedly blowing many people to pieces, what God these poor people were praying to during their last few moments of life and whether or not it was the same God the Chaplain prayed to. He used to say we were doing God's work but I always wondered about the other side. I also wondered why was I spared. I further did not understand how aggression got placed into the soul of man, if we were created in the image of God. If there were a God I could not believe that it was His intent to create men as they are. Most of the ills of man have been perpetuated by some form of religious philosophy that requires that you either believe as we do or you will be killed.

If you disagree with this you only need look at the inquisition that began in 1233 and really became apparent by 1542, when absolute repression, torture and church sanctioned murder was committed all in the name of God. To answer the aggression question, my hypothesis is as follows: One day, one of our early ancestors flung a rock at an animal, accidentally striking it in the head and killing it. This was an amazing feat and he started throwing rocks at anything that moved and became quite skillful. The young men in his tribe admired him greatly and wanted to be like him. He became a leader and soon had a following, all becoming expert rock throwers. This was long before the ten commandments were written, one of which states, "Thou shall not covet thy neighbors wife,"; but, covet they did. One day their leader suggested that they gather up a handful of good throwing rocks and travel some distance to another tribe. They attacked the tribe and easily put the men who survived to flight and coveted to their heart's content. Their leader became a dictator with a large following, going across the land pillaging, destroying, and coveting without resistance.

One day they encountered a tribe where one member had found out that if he took two strips of hide with a pocket tied to each end, put a rock in the pocket, he could swing it around over his head, let it fly with much more force and distance. It was called a slingshot. Our rock throwers were repelled by a barrage of rocks and the new aggressors were out of our rock thrower's range. Thus, the arms race was started and has not stopped yet. I'm sure you would agree that you are just as dead being hit in the head with a rock as you would be if hit by a missile capable of hitting a target from a thousand miles away.

Now here we have tribes becoming countries and with this progression, various objects were held up for worship, such as the sun, moon, earth and all forms of mythical or stone idols. Their idols did not satisfy the fear that man felt of the unknown, so supreme deities were created with each culture interpreting their deity in different ways and with different names. Massive military complexes were created in an arms race to enforce the different country's beliefs. So now, I will again ask the question, "When I was instrumental in bombing people, what God were they praying to?" The final conclusion I've come to is that less than five percent of the world's population are in military service and in a position to end civilization as we know it. Thus, perhaps in the final throes of annihilation, either by nuclear or biological warfare, a mutant form will emerge without hands, unable to throw a rock.

Many of my friends died a terrible, fiery death and many of them were devout Christians. Yet here I was alive with a loving wife, a daughter and now a son wondering what the future held. Also I had to accept this as fate and believe that maybe it will compensate somewhat, for the lonely years. I decided to leave the rest of it up to fate also. I was a pretty good crap shooter while overseas and since there were so many kids who had never played, I was able to send money home plus most of my regular pay. We also got three hundred dollars discharge pay. There were no houses to rent in Boise, but we finally found a farm house about ten miles from town.

A great disservice was done to the returning World War I veterans. Their jobs had been taken by others and many of them had suffered serious injuries, including being gassed, which destroyed their health. Bonuses had been promised, but they were not being paid. The veterans finally marched on Washington, D.C., camped on the grounds near the Capitol Building, and were harassed by their own government. The World War I veterans then decided to get legislation passed to help and protect the returning veterans in the future. Their efforts helped create the G.I. Bill, which gave veterans the right to their former jobs, educational benefits and government guaranteed home loans. Millions of returning veterans owed a tremendous debt of gratitude to these World War I veterans, who helped make these benefits available.

I applied for and got a six thousand dollar G.I. loan. I took the building contract myself, hired a couple of carpenters to help, and built a house with a full basement. I shoveled every pound of sand, gravel and cement into a half yard mixer in order to pour the basement. We moved into the basement before the upstairs was finished. Then I went to work for Mountain States Telephone and Telegraph Company, affectionately known as "Ma Bell", in August of 1946 for thirty one dollars a week. The payments on the house were about fifty dollars a month. I could have made that much a day working in construction. I knew it would be tough, but also knew it was what I had to have. I had gone to work for Ma Bell in August of 1946 and worked evenings and weekends to finish our new home. We had used some of the loan money to live on and as a result didn't have enough money left to install a furnace. It broke our hearts but we had to sell our beloved Chevy car to buy the furnace. This caused me to have to catch a bus to get to work.

It was a tough winter and on April 6, 1947 two things happened. The telephone company went on strike and our second son, Stanley was born. I believed in unions so I walked on the picket line with the other employees until finally we were broke. I had no choice but to find a job in order to pay the house payments and buy food. A dam was being built on the Payette River at Cascade, Idaho. Cascade was a small logging town about eighty miles north of Boise. I got a job running a D-8 caterpillar tractor and got a room in the Chief Hotel, where I stayed during the week, only going home on the weekends. The strike lasted almost six weeks; and even though I was making as much money per day as "Ma Bell" was paying me in a week, being away from Lorraine and the children further convinced me that construction jobs taking me away from my family were not what I needed. Soon after this I became a line foreman at the telephone company and had a crew of my own to supervise.

Lorraine's brother, Louis had graduated from medical school and was working for the United States Public Health Service. He had been assigned to Boise in charge of the Venereal Disease program. Field men were sent out to check the girls in the houses of prostitution to make sure that they were free of venereal diseases. Also, any cases of syphilis or gonorrhea that were found had to be diligently followed up on to prevent any further spread of the disease. My brother-in-law eventually managed to close most of the houses of prostitution in Boise; but I was always careful never to let anyone know that he was my relative because this did not endear him to many men. He had married a nurse named Jenny, had a baby girl and was almost as poor as we were; so they moved into the basement of our house, paid us rent, shared grocery costs and both families benefited.

I liked my job and was getting better wages. The time passed quickly and our third son Robert was born September 30, 1948. Our earlier plans of a daughter first, then three boys had become a reality, which proved the power of positive thinking. Lorraine had graduated from college with a degree in chemistry and a minor in mathematics, so got a job teaching school in the fall of 1949. Things were looking good.

One day my crew was working down a rural road and I had to talk to a lady at a small farm house about trimming one of her trees so it wouldn't touch the telephone line. She invited me in and we sat in a nice, warm cozy kitchen and got to talking. Her only son had been killed in the war; her husband had died and she was going to have to sell her place. It was twelve acres all in peach and apple trees, about an acre of raspberry bushes, and some pasture. She said that many realtors wanted to buy the place, but she hoped to sell it to a family who would enjoy it as much as her family had. When I told her we had a daughter and three rambunctious boys trying to live in a small house, she said she would sell it to me for eighteen thousand dollars, with five thousand dollars down and the balance at six percent. I brought Lorraine and the kids out that evening and all of us got very excited and wanted it very much. With the security of working for the telephone company and being a supervisor and Lorraine able to teach school or substitute we had no trouble getting a loan for the five thousand down payment. We had thirty days to close, so we put our house up for sale. A buyer assumed our mortgage and paid us forty dollars a month above our loans, and in May of 1952, we moved to our farm. It was a year of no frost and all the fruit trees were loaded and the lady who sold us the place was delighted with our family and had gone to live with her daughter in town. She came out quite often to teach us how to irrigate and take care of the trees. People had bought fruit from her for years so when it was ripe we all picked fruit, filling bushel baskets, and brought them up to the yard where we sold them as fast as we could pick.

Our peach crop.

We had about an acre of raspberry bushes and hired some ladies to pick the ripe berries. The money just rolled in. I just couldn't believe it and had visions of quitting Ma Bell and making a living selling fruit. It was a good thing I didn't quit, because it was the last year we didn't have frost when the trees were in bloom. Over the years close to a thousand used tires had been accumulated. If frost were predicted these old tires were placed down between the rows of trees, where they were ready to be set on fire if the temperature dropped close to 28 degrees. The fruit buds would be killed at this temperature. This was a standard procedure, used in most orchards, and some mornings the skies had a pall of smoke throughout the valley from burning tires.

One day a man came in with a truck and asked if he could look through our tires. He was looking for any tire that could be recapped. He offered me two tires for each one he took. This was a good deal for me, so I told him to have at it. I found out later that he was looking for 600-16 tires and was easily getting five or six dollars apiece for them. This was a standard size tire for most cars at that time and since hardly any tires had been made during the war, this size was in great demand.

Even with the tires, some years we lost all the fruit or a good portion of it and never had a year like the first one. The benefits of the farm far exceeded the losses though, as the boys had a horse to ride, were given chores to do and since I had bought a milk cow, each of them had to learn to milk. They hated it; but it was teaching them responsibility and the milk was good for us all, and the pure cream made the best home made ice cream in the world. I made a deal with a dairy man to buy his bull calves since they were of little use to him. I told the boys if they fed the calves until they ate grass and could be sold for meat, that I would give them the profits from every tenth calf. Years later they accused me of only buying nineteen calves, then quitting.

I liked my job with Ma Bell. Kay was growing into a young woman and the boys were getting big and healthy. We used to wrestle a lot. They would pile on me and I could toss them off until one day they pinned me to the floor. I was spread-eagled and couldn't move. That ended that.

I wanted to go fishing. This in itself was not startling and certainly nothing new. As a native of Idaho, to borrow and aptly apply a cliche, most of us learned to fish before we learned to walk. This was probably a slight exaggeration, but the point was valid. No, this fishing was different. For years, I had longed to take the time and have the money to make the six hundred mile trip to the mouth of the mighty Columbia River at Ilwaco,

Washington, go out into the Pacific Ocean and fish for salmon. Time after time, the more fortunate of my hunting and fishing friends had done this and come back with a certain amount of superior embellishments talking about how wonderful it had been. I had been forced to listen to these accounts of their individual exploits, the tremendous size of the fish they had caught, and the exceptional skill used to land these monsters. I always listened with a feigned enthusiasm, making appropriate remarks; while at the same time the hypocritical, envious side of me would be wishing that they had been pulled over-board and maybe not completely drowned, but at least have ended up with no fish and a sore throat so bad that they couldn't talk for a week.

My family liked seafood, so we bought fish quite often. Using this fact as a psychological peg to hang my hopes on, I began to plan my strategy, so as to come up with a justification for going. This was some month to six weeks before the normal salmon run started. Lorraine was not stupid and any illogical or impractical maneuvers on my part would have been met with a high degree of intelligent argument. Seemingly sound ideas in the past had been seen through immediately and held up for ridicule, to the extent that, by now, I realized if I were going to pull this one off, it would require much more than mediocre effort.

Lorraine did love me though and tried to cater to my needs and wants, so when I started expressing a desire for seafood she fell for strategy number one. Not taking any chances, I requested halibut. Then after three or four meals of this, I mildly remarked one evening, that the meal was excellent but that a change would be nice, maybe salmon. The trip had become an all consuming campaign with me by now and like a skier, instead of "think snow!" slogans, I was subconsciously saying to myself, "think salmon!"

And think salmon I did. Not only did I think salmon but I ate salmon and I ate it with great gusto, even two and three helpings at a meal. Nothing would snow my wife quicker than appreciative remarks about her cooking. Her natural, suspicious nature would be bridged by this one thing.

My three sons and daughter attempted to protest salmon again at one meal, but since they were at the helpless age where I could still bluff them, it only took a very stern "Shut up, and eat the food your mother has spent two hours cooking!" to forestall this small threat. I was even sustained in this one by their mother who uttered an appropriate "Yeah!"

Salmon sold in our area for about three dollars a pound and up. Long before the first month of my six weeks plan was up, our meat allotment from the family budget was almost gone. Now, Lorraine was put in the position of continuing to take the short cut to my heart via my stomach or dropping back to hamburger and wieners, which I did not like. I had anticipated this situation correctly and on the salmon meals had knocked myself out with pretenses of appreciation and gluttony. I secretly hoped things would come to a head soon because I was having betraying thoughts about ever wanting to see another salmon, much less eat it, and this worried me.

Strategy number two came into play even sooner than I had anticipated. In fact, with a whole week left in the first month's plan, we had a family conference. In fairness, family conferences were not too frequent and were always held after the children were in bed and during the precious hour or two left from the day. During this time, sometimes I heard a little gossip, usually about some other woman in the neighborhood; and even though the tale would be recounted with outraged vehemence, it usually did have salacious undertones so that I could sit and listen to it with some degree of pleasant conjecture.

Generally though, the conferences consisted of much income manipulating, with sums juggled from one charge account to another. I'm reminded of a joke I once read about a family budget. In this one they put all their monthly bills in a fish bowl, spent what they wished and then if there were any money left they took a bill out of the bowl and paid it. If any store felt put out by this method, they simply left his bill out of the bowl completely. This was probably as good a way as any, because with the best of planning and conscientious endeavor on our part, we ended up each month broke, with bills left unpaid.

Tonight's conference was on money; no erring wives, but just a simple statement of fact that the grocery allowance was gone. This was said with some bewilderment by Lorraine, because she did try. I felt a small twinge of conscience at this point, but easily suppressed it, and manifested shocked disbelief at this previously unheard of thing. With tears in her eyes, she explained that she felt that since I was a good husband and father and worked so hard that I, at least, deserved to get the food that I liked. She went on to explain that she had been buying higher priced meat than usual this month and as a result of this extravagance was now out of money.

Strategy number three! At this point a bigger person, and one not so determined, and even possibly not as devious, would have been magnanimous about the whole thing and comforted her with some soothing comment of indifference as to what was to be served at mealtimes. But, I had gone too far, and eaten too much fish to weaken. After fifteen years of marriage, a melancholy face was not hard to achieve; I immediately displayed this, while at the same time agreeing with her earlier statement about being a good and true hard working husband. With the absolute touch of a self styled genius I mentioned that all my friends seemed to at least get what they liked to eat; and were even able, at times, to indulge in alcoholic orgies, with no telling how many amorous opportunities to tempt them, as these two vices were compatible. After having said this self-serving line, I tapered it off by saying that I did none of those things, and was lucky if I even got to go hunting or fishing for a weekend.

In a tone of voice that almost brought tears to my own eyes, I closed the conversation by stating that from a practical standpoint, the institution of marriage and family responsibilities left a lot to be desired; and querulously questioned why any man continued to knock himself out for no apparent reason. With this I got up, placed my hand on the small of my back, gave a heart rending sigh, and with shoulders bowed, went to bed. I felt the secret here was not to talk too much.

The next morning I was deliberately slow in getting up, and after shaving and dressing and entering the kitchen, assumed a quiet and reflective look. I thoroughly enjoyed bacon and eggs and probably haven't missed eating them five days out of any given seven, for the past fifteen years. But this morning I pushed them around on my plate, with pauses during which I gazed off into the distance, as though conjuring up visions of a tropical island paradise inhabited by luscious maidens. Then, with my breakfast half eaten, I pushed the plate back, stated that I guessed that I had better join the rat race, and with no further comment left for work.

I must mention here that all of this was not an easy thing to do. I was not a man without some degree of integrity. And yet, as I drove along the familiar route to my job; the base motives that were inherent in all men, and only suppressed by a thin veneer of civilization, rose to the surface and as I reflected on my actions and assessed their effect on my wife, I had the perverse satisfaction of feeling that the stage had been set. That evening when I got home everything seemed in its normal state of confusion. Three healthy boys less than two years apart were running through the house. My daughter, being the oldest, was helping her mother in the kitchen and had assumed her long suffering look of complete disdain for her brothers, cooking and life.

I only became aware of something strange when we were at the table. I gradually became conscious of the fact that my wife was filled with a suppressed excitement. Her conversation was just a shade loud and her face was slightly flushed with animation. This awareness on my part was felt throughout the evening, which finally reached its end. The children were in bed and I was sitting in my usual brown chair, when a fresh cup of coffee was put in front of me, and I felt her warm and faithful arm around my shoulders. At the same time, she dropped a common white envelope in my lap. Assuming a surprised look I opened it; and was then truly surprised to find a brand new one hundred dollar bill inside.

In response to my reaction and with true love and joy shining from her eyes, she told me that she had been doing a lot of thinking. She had arrived at two conclusions. One, that I liked fish and it sold for three dollars and six cents a pound; and secondly, she knew I had always wanted to go salmon fishing. With a great deal of pride, she showed me figures that proved that if I went fishing, brought home some fresh fish and had the others canned, we could actually save money. She had drawn the one hundred dollars from our meager, untouchable savings account, for me to make the trip.

I naturally displayed the appropriate amount of doubt as to the merits of this conclusion on her part; and after a decent interval, during which she became emphatic that this was the only thing to do, I finally gave in, kissed her lightly on the cheek, complimented her on her business sense and womanly wisdom and hurried outside. It was necessary for me to go out-side where without being seen, I could allow my expression to reflect my feelings. They would have been a dead giveaway because I had based the whole plan on strategy number four, for which I also had figures, and after having built the psychological background had intended to present them as a clincher, and hope for the best.

This had appeared to me to be the toughest part and now suddenly everything had fallen into place beautifully, with all of strategy number four having been literally dumped into my lap. It was a fine, warm summer evening as I stood gazing into the infinitesimal vastness of the sky, I already had visions of giant salmon leaping again and again at the end of my line. I could see their iridescent sides shimmering and glistening in the sun, and the water spraying upward like jewels as they fell back into the sea. And yet, though I had outsmarted my wife and should have been happy, I already knew that I wouldn't go. Maybe someday when our job was finished she and I would go together. In the meantime the ocean wouldn't go away; it is just as lasting and indestructible as what was waiting for me back in my home.

Four or five years later I did get to go fishing. A good neighbor and friend, Jack Richards, owned a Bonanza airplane. Jack, Kenny Stower, Tom Powers and I were invited to go to the coast and stay with a former Boise man, who had a boat and was living at Ilwaco, Washington, at the mouth of the Columbia River. The fishing was great and we all got our limit before heading home. We were flying at about 2500 feet altitude when a valve broke and went through the side of the engine. We were just opposite Portland, Oregon, across the Columbia River. Jack immediately called the tower informing them of our position and telling them that we were going down. I had promised myself that I would never fly again, but Jack had been a fighter pilot during the great war, and had received a serious wound to his stomach. He had held his guts together with one hand and managed to return to base. This was the story I had heard, not from Jack though, because like most veterans who actually saw the horrors of war, he refused to talk about it.

Anyway, assuming it was true, I felt that he could handle most any emergency. This proved to be true as he managed to get under high power lines coming across from the power dam on the Columbia River. This was a four passenger plane and I was sitting in the front with Jack. Since it was obvious that we had to go down, I told Kenny and Tom to tighten their seat belts, cross their arms on the back of the seats and press their head tightly against their arms. I did the same but couldn't help sneaking a look to see what might be my last look at life. Jack had immediately picked a field, maneuvered the plane, and made a smooth, dead engine landing in a mint field. Mint fields were sub-irrigated, so there were no ditches. We rolled on mint for several hundred feet before finally stopping. There was a strong smell of fresh mint, which possibly covered up worse odors. The owner was immediately there in his pickup to help us. None of us got a scratch.

All of our equipment and salmon were saved, except for one big fish that we gave to the farmer. We rolled the fish into our sleeping bags and caught a plane home to Boise. Jack went back later, had a new engine put into the plane and flew it out of the field. Had the engine trouble happened thirty minutes later, we would have been over the John Day country in Oregon, where huge boulders dot the landscape. I took all the fish to a cold storage locker, had them cut up and frozen, then took a share to Kenny and Tom. At Jack's house, I took his share in and sat down for awhile to visit. When I went out to the pickup, half the cats in the country were in the back of the truck chewing on my share of the salmon. But, at least, I had survived another plane crash!

I would like to recall for you an association with Kenny Stower, one of the men who went fishing with us. Kenny worked for the telephone company, also, with over 25 years as a right-of-way engineer. He had a farm north of Eagle and over the years, he and I had built up a good hunting outfit. We were close friends and knew that we could rely on each other, if one got lost while hunting or any other situation. I liked to drive the pickup pulling our horse trailer, so when we got to Lowman, Idaho and were headed to Bear Valley, we stopped and got a six pack of beer. Kenny didn't drink and I had just assumed he didn't like the stuff. He opened a can of beer for me, then surprised me when he opened another can for himself. We made another stop or two, buying more beer and when we finally got to Bear Valley, neither of us could hit the ground with our hat.

Poor Kenny could never stop. After that he had bottles hidden all over his home and farm. He started missing work. I would go out and make some coffee and food for him. I took him to Alcoholics Anonymous meetings, but nothing helped. He lost his farm, his wife and daughter and the telephone company with much regret had to let him go. I have drunk moderately all my life and the last thing I would need the next morning was another drink. Kenny would cry, knowing what he was doing but he seemed helpless to stop. I had always had a contempt for a drunk and felt that a good kick in the ass would have straightened him out.

My good friend committed suicide from despair. I have learned to have a lot more empathy for anyone who is cursed with this particular affliction.

We bought a good inboard boat and spent many week ends and evenings at Lucky Peak Reservoir, a short distance from our house, having picnics and boating with our friends. We all water skied, even Lorraine and as the boat was docked at the reservoir, the children and their friends spent hours having fun. It turned out to be the best family entertainment we could have had. One year the local Lion's Club held a water skiing contest and my three boys won a good share of the trophies.

All of our children were active in music and sports. We bought Kay a Haines silver, open hole flute, which she played in the band and orchestra She accepted a scholarship in music at Wichita State University in Kansas and left on the train in September of 1960. Lorraine cried all day and her going left a void in the family. I got a little weepy also because she was our first born and I missed her. Lorraine had the same dedication to education as her mother had had; and when Steve's grades were not the greatest I suggested maybe he should enter a vocational program and learn a trade. I never made that mistake again as I was informed in no uncertain terms that she hadn't fed him and wiped his bottom for him to not get an education. She then went to the school to find out what the trouble was and was informed he had a good mind but was stubborn especially in Physics where he questioned everything, wanting to find out why a fulcrum could not raise the world if long enough. Some of the girls were learning by rote and getting A's, but had no practical understanding of the material.

Steve graduated from High school in 1963 and entered the University of Idaho that fall to study engineering, then transferred to Brigham Young University in Provo, Utah. Stan graduated in 1965 and followed his brother to B.Y.U. Each graduated from B.Y.U., Steve as a geologic engineer and Stan with a degree in Business Administration.

In the meantime Kay had changed from music to a degrees in psychology and English. By coincidence, our daughter, Kay, after finishing college, worked at the Children's Home in Boise where I had lived as a child. I asked her to write a few words about her experiences that summer. This was her reply.

"It was my first job out of college, and it was at the Children's Home. I had to be there at six o'clock in the morning. In Boise, in those days, it meant temperatures in the 40's even though by mid-day it would be in the 90's. I would drive to the Children's Home in the crisp summer mornings, with the smell of lilacs still lingering in the air, and I would think about my Father, who had lived at the Children's Home when he was a boy. As I herded my charges through their daily activities, I would often look at the old corridors and rooms and picture my Dad there as a child. So much hurt, so much pain, so many children! Sometime I would hear the voices echoing off the walls.

My Dad wouldn't talk to me about it much in those days, but I know this —it made me a better person. I knew that I would never have hurt one of those kids, the way my Dad was hurt, and I think it's part of the reason why I ended up spending my life working with children. Life, . . . it has a way, as the saying goes, "everything that goes around, comes around."

After working in Boise at the Children's Home until fall, she enrolled at Case Western University in Cleveland, Ohio for a Master's degree in Social Work. While in Cleveland she met a fine young man, whom she married. It is true that she did dedicate her life to working with children, finally obtaining a Doctor of Philosophy degree in Adult Education and is presently Programs Division Manager at the Juvenile Court in Boise, Idaho.

This left Bob at home, and in later years he would say he never had it so good, and should never have left home. It was probably true as now "The Mother" who had spread her energy over the six of us was now down to two. I didn't gain much benefit because I was like an old shoe, but the youngest child got a lot of attention. He graduated in 1966 from high school and being a good athlete, had a basketball scholarship to Utah State University in Logan, Utah.

CHAPTER 10
THE GOLDEN YEARS

THE FAMILY

How often do we sit
At the table of Life
Thinking it looks so bare
Only picking up crumbs
From the floor
Wondering if anyone cares

Who decides who eats
From this table
Loaded with fame and fortune
We all are equally able
But we never take a seat
Like a sacrificial lamb
Only stand and bleat.

Then someone said
Go look at your table
What do you see there
You see a wife
Children and great grandchildren
everywhere
All healthy and able
Go then take a seat
And eat from the food of life
Yours is a wonderful table.

Of all the events that have happened in my life, the most gratifying has been, of course, my association and eventual marriage to Lorraine. The second event, was being invited to join The Poachers Club. The membership included many professional men in Boise and leaders in Federal agencies responsible for wildlife management. The first meetings started as early as 1938. Homer Martin, one of the founders said many times, "No one has enough money to buy a membership; no one is too poor to belong." Included in the membership are a Governor of our State, Supreme Court Justice, and all Fish and Game directors and their assistants and U.S. Forrest Service and B.L.M. personnel. I was asked to join in 1969 and was privileged to associate with the finest group of men who ever came together. They were not pretentious and had no axes to grind, at least in this group there was tremendous respect for one another.

The initial goal for the founders of the club was to take the Idaho Department of Fish and Game out of politics and to avoid changing personnel with each change of government. The name, "Poachers Club" came from a remark made by the State Fish and Game Warden, W.R. McIntyre, who stated, "There's a bunch of poaching sons-of-bitches down there in Boise, who are trying to do away with my job!" Judge Koelsch urged that the group adopt the name "Poachers" and always greet one another as "Sons-of-Bitches." It was approved and is still the custom to this day. The Club basically concerned itself with conservation and the environment. It still has many members who belong to the Idaho Wildlife Federation and other groups devoted to wildlife.

All members carry a "Poachers Card." If a member does not show his card, he becomes obligated to donate a fifth of quality spirits to the Club. I've had many years of good times and great friendships with this group. The club's motto is "Happy days and sunny skies and Laeng Mae Veer Lumm Reek", interpreted as "long may your chimney smoke."

Lorraine and I got up one morning and the house was empty. We were more glad than sad as each of us had presented a united front in discipline, supported all the children's' activities, had many wonderful hunting trips for me and the boys and a home for the most part full of love and laughter; but now we could plan for the two of us and we felt that we had done a good job and were ready for a new life together. I had worked for the telephone company as a construction foreman for eighteen years. As a working man, it was a good job. The sick benefits were better than most major companies; but unless I were to get an advancement or change of some kind the thought of putting in another twenty years was beginning to bother me. Down through the years I had come up with schemes for our acreage including trailer parks, storage sheds, and with all the fruit, even a public cannery. The need for a steady income took precedence over all these ideas, yet the desire was still there.

But now with the children gone, this desire started eating on me and was getting reinforced daily from the boredom of my job, plus the unfortunate circumstance of being at odds with a new construction superintendent. Sometimes men will feel a sense of animosity toward each other; so it was in my case. I suppose having done the same job for so long, I displayed an attitude of independence, seemingly not catering to or respecting his position. A remark made by him and relayed to me was, "I'm going to run him out of the company." Also, in fairness, I must accept the fact that I had a psychological chip on my shoulder and reacted to any criticism from a familiar lifetime of rejection. This complex allowed me to wallow in self pity or martyrdom, which was the only role I had ever felt comfortable with. Cynicism about the underlying motives of any association with another person was so ingrained in my mind, that it sometimes caused conflict in my jobs and even with Lorraine. At times, I would get my feelings hurt over some slight, real or imaginary, and pout for a couple of depressing days. It had become my only refuge, which was hard for anyone to understand. With my conflict with the new construction superintendent, something had to give. It was scary to even think about giving up all the security and benefits of the telephone company to gamble on a new venture, yet I felt I had to try. Lorraine had gone to work in 1956 as a microbiologist with the Idaho Department of Public Health Laboratories and had advanced to a position that paid an excellent salary.

We discussed this over and over. I was afraid that if I failed to develop a business, then finding another good job would be impossible at my age. I couldn't put it out of my mind and it began to affect my job and also my health. So one night when Lorraine saw me rubbing my arm, she simply said, "Tomorrow, give the company your notice, gather up your things, and come home." So I did. God bless her!

Of all the ideas I'd had, the one I felt the strongest about was a rental project. We would design the ground as a planned unit development with houses surrounding a park in the center with a swimming pool, cabanas with barbecues, a small putting green, shuffle board and even horseshoe pitching. All of the houses would be on a one year lease, including all utilities except telephone. All maintenance would be provided, lawn mow-ing and watering. Tenants would be free of all these demands.

We would cater to busy executives, being transferred in but not wanting to buy, yet needing the privacy of a home. Children would be restricted to sixteen years of age or older. All appliances would be provided, including air conditioners. Carpet and drapes would be installed. If a tenant did not have furniture, a source for complete rental furniture would be available. The more I thought about this plan, the more excited I got, being sure it would work. Taking a plat of our ground to an engineering firm, I explained the design including the park and amenities but told them I couldn't pay until it was finished. Their business was slow at the time and with our excellent credit rating they agreed.

With this I went to a local artist, who did a fine color picture, two by two and a half feet showing the center park, pool, putting green, and shuffle board, surrounded by twenty one houses. All of this was in a setting of green grass and trees. We're ready now to find financing. Hopefully starting out with a picture worth a thousand words.

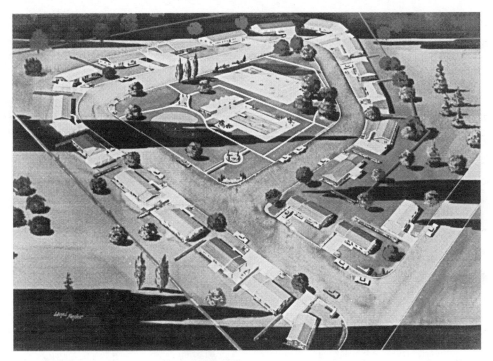

Hill Park Homes

The Boise Cascade Company had just opened a component home factory in Meridian about ten miles from Boise. They were capable of building a finished home which could then be transported by truck to a foundation. I met with the manager of the Meridian plant three different times. Finally he said, "You are so damn persistent, I guess we will work with you." If I could get financing they would sell me twenty one houses, eleven of which would be three bedrooms and ten two bedrooms. A sale price was agreed on and Lorraine and I signed the contract. I had the cost for the engineering and now went to a local contractor, who gave me a bid for putting in the streets. I also got a firm bid per yard on the concrete. We then added ten percent for miscellaneous expenses and with Lorraine's help we arrived at a final proposed cost. We had also worked up figures showing that this house could be rented for far less than ownership, when considering taxes, interest and all other expenses.

Each morning with few exceptions I took Lorraine to work, then spent the day meeting with bankers, who had to present the plan to their boards for approval. I believed in the concept so thoroughly and my enthusiasm was a big factor in their considering it. I had not only visited with all the local institutions but had contacted any out of State possibilities. The word started coming back that while most thought the concept had much merit but nothing like this had been done before and they had nothing to use as a base, in comparison. Because they dealt with investors' money, they didn't feel that they could risk it. After about six months of this, I began to get discouraged and felt that I was letting my wife support me while I sat at home. Each time I mentioned that maybe I should get a job Lorraine got mad; said that I had always wanted to do something besides work for a living, and to get the hell out there and do it. So I did and one fine day I had an appointment with the president of Intermountain Gas Company. With a nice leather brief case in my hand that my brother in-law, Louis had given me, I kept the appointment. The president of the company asked, "What do you have in that brief case?" I got the impression he felt I was wasting his time so replied, "Actually it's just for looks and all I have in here is a ham sandwich and if I can bum a cup of coffee I'll eat my lunch." Perhaps he had come out of the depression also, and recognized the phrase. In any case he grinned and motioned me into his office.

I sat my picture on a chair in plain view and went into my pitch. I had said it so many times it was perfected and to the point. After asking a few questions I could answer with sincerity he picked up his phone, called the bank in Boise and made something like the following statement. "There's a man in my office with a new concept of a housing project that I think will work. He needs $270,000. Draw up all the proper papers and Intermountain Gas Company will co-sign his loan." That evening I couldn't wait to tell Lorraine. I knew she was as excited as I was but merely said, "Well, it doesn't surprise me. I knew you would do it."

Three days later we walked into the bank and signed a signature loan for $270,000 walked across the street to a coffee shop, sat down, not quite sure if it were not a dream. We had borrowed $20,000 from the credit union to remodel the old farm house, had four children's college debt to help pay off, and with a stroke of a pen were now almost $300,000 in debt.

It was my finest hour and dream or not I was more than ready to get started. This was to be a total gas project and would be a show place for the gas company. One of their managers Denny Yost was a great help in giving me advice and helping me in purchasing all the appliances, including three ton air conditioners for each house. I owed him a great debt of gratitude. The houses were all the same size with different floor plans. This made it much easier to set up the foundation forms, using the same pattern for each location. I had the clearance dug for setting up these forms after first pouring an eight by sixteen inch footing, that was square with the lot lines and absolutely level. On this was set two foot high by eight foot long sections of forms and filled to the level top with concrete, and then stripped and moved to the next lot. I was a perfectionist and each foundation was perfectly square and level.

As each foundation was ready Boise Cascade moved the completely finished house to the foundation. A local house mover, Bill moved the houses to the site. I knew him quite well from working with him in raising telephone lines. The first house he set on the foundation was an inch or two not square on the corners. He said, "Does that look O.K.?" In plain words I told him those foundations were square and level so put the blankety blank house on it the same way. He just grinned and every house from then on fit perfectly. I would see Lorraine off the work and couldn't wait to get back to the project. It was a labor of love working for myself. I put in the septic tanks and drain fields then hired a plumber to run the sewage drains from the house. He also hooked up the water. Our good friends who owned a fine furniture company, installed the carpets and drapes and the houses were ready to move into. The swimming pool, cabanas, putting green along with gas barbecues, and horseshoe pits were all being finished.

Everything was done except the carports and the landscaping. My son, Bob was home part of the time and helped install a carport on each house. Hans Babbit, who owned one of the local nurseries was in the process of moving to a new location, so he made me a good deal to completely land-scape the project. It was good for both of us because when the plants and trees were dug up they could be planted here instead of at the new location. This left the grass. Stan was home also, and we put in hundreds of feet of sprinkler pipe, planted grass seed and the project was almost finished. I was glad to see it done. I had dropped from over two hundred pounds in weight to around one hundred eighty pounds and was in better shape than I had been in years. The boys found this out when I challenged them to an arm wrestling match. I had been swinging a four pound hammer, setting up forms and shoveling gravel, while they had been sitting in college and they didn't have a chance.

The gas company was making this a showplace for their gas appliances and had two thousand color brochures printed showing all the amenities. A full page advertisement was put in our local paper announcing a grand open house. Some of the gas company employees acted as hosts and it seemed like half the city of Boise came to look at the project. The concept was a huge success and soon all houses were leased. What had been our dream was now an overwhelming reality. There were enough musicians living in the project to form our own four or five piece band. We had potluck dinners around the pool, horseshoe pitching contests and once put on a three day luau with a whole pig cooking in a pit, and barbecued salmon. Platforms were built surrounded by palm trees with Hawaiian dancers. The place was gaining a great reputation as a fun filled, no mainte-nance life style and we could almost require an application from prospective tenants. We wanted no do-gooders . We did want people who would take a drink in moderation and enjoyed a good story. We were such popular landlords that small problems were usually taken care of by the tenants rather than bother us. Lorraine decided to quit her job after thirteen years with the Health Department and I welcomed her home with open arms.

I was so proud of her and so glad that the way things were going it looked like neither of us would ever have to work again. Especially Lorraine, who had allowed my dream to come true with absolute faith and encouragement, along with her working to make it possible.

We had almost six years of the ego satisfaction of being owners and managers of this fine project and now had lenders coming to us willing to loan us money to develop anything we wanted. We did consider other ideas, such as storage sheds as there were none in the valley. One day a group of investors offered us what seemed like a fortune for the project. After twenty five years of raising and educating the children plus doing the development we felt we had earned a rest. We sold out, gave the children any furniture they wanted, had a yard sale, and bought an Airstream travel trailer with a Chevy suburban to pull it. We joined the Airstream Wally Byam Club and signed up for a tour of Mexico. One glorious day we left town like a couple of kids, with everything we owned in the trailer, no telephones, no grass to cut, and free as a bird to head south. How sweet it was! It was the first week of December 1970 before all the paper work was completed and we could leave. The roads were snow covered and our first experience in pulling a travel trailer was an interesting challenge. My past ability to drive trucks and heavy equipment made this more of a fun thing than a worry.

We made our way through Nevada to Reno, then on to Sacramento, California where our son Steve lived with his family. He had married and now had three children, two boys and a girl. We spent a pleasant week with our trailer parked in their driveway getting acquainted with these grand-children. We were to rendezvous with the Wally Byam caravan the middle of January at Tucson, Arizona. We left Sacramento and took our time getting there. Before we left for Mexico we were briefed on the rules of the caravan and the places where we would stop. It sounded like great fun. We were excited about getting started.

On January 20, 1971, two hundred eighty trailers left Tucson heading through Mexico, stopping at all the major cities along the way. We had volunteered to work on the parking crew, which turned out to be one of the best parts of our trip. The six couples on the crew always left one day ahead of the main group to mark the next parking field with line stripes. The next day as the trailers arrived we directed them with red flags to a parking space. One of the couples was employees of the club and had gone on the route many times and also spoke fluent Spanish. They knew all the best places for entertainment and food. After marking the field, we would all spend the evening enjoying these places.

One of the places was the world famous Shrimp Bucket Restaurant at Mazatlan. The night before leaving Boise we had a farewell dinner with some close friends. While waiting to be seated at the Shrimp Bucket these friends had finished eating and came out the door of the restaurant. It was quite a coincidence to see them some four thousand miles from home.

All in all it was a great trip with each stop having entertainment or sight seeing tours. One was to a tequila bottling plant where we were entertained by mariachi bands and free margaritas. It was one of the happiest stops. We arrived in Acapulco on February 20th and had dinner two different times sitting on the balcony above the rocks where the Mexican divers, cross themselves and then dive into that narrow cleft into the ocean. You have to admire the courage it must take to do this, crossing themselves or not, since their guardian angel might have been distracted at that moment.

The caravan was going back to the States from Acapulco, but we had no reason to get back so we decided to stay. We found a trailer park less than a quarter of a mile from the bay with full hook-ups for two dollars a day. We could walk past the big hotels with their one hundred dollar a night rooms, sit on the beach or have a drink in one of their bars. We felt no envy knowing our adventure was more fun. We had made many friends from the caravan, especially the parking crew and kept in touch with them for many years.

Another advantage of pulling the trailer was having our own transportation. We spent many days exploring the area and visiting the many points of interest. One of these was a red-light district about five miles above town. It was a unique place with dozens of girls circulating amongst the tables in a large open area. Mainly it catered to the men from the many ships that anchored in the bay. Lots of Naval ships from all over the world came into the port. You could sit at one of the tables, order a beer and food then be entertained by a mariachi band and watch the girls. One girl came and sat on my lap, which only caused my smart aleck wife to just laugh. It almost hurt my feelings. Watching these young Mexican girls my mind drifted back to the time Dick, Paul and I used to spend some of our hard earned money from picking hops. How long ago it seems.

The time had come to leave for the States, but we stopped in Mexico City for a few days. We hired a taxi driver to show us the sights. One of the most interesting places were the pyramids to the sun and the moon built many years before. They were still in the process of excavating the city that surrounded the pyramids. From Mexico City we drove to the border and entered the United States at McAllen, Texas. What a contrast it was. On the Mexico side the people were living in poverty, their homes were shacks with dirt floors. Dozens of naked kids ran around with goats, dogs and chickens. Just across the border, an imaginary line were nice homes, paved streets and well kept yards with everything clean. It was the same type soil and the same climate so why the difference. Some have said that it's the lack of available credit, which the Americans have to buy homes and cars, if gainfully employed.

My own assessment after seeing the poverty that exists all over Mexico is that the domination of the Catholic church that has held its people in bondage. I saw the same thing in Italy during the war. Most of the towns, small and large, had a church. Some of the churches were quite affluent and provided a home for the priests and nuns, who seemingly lived pretty good compared to the surrounding poverty. It appeared as though the peons had only one purpose in life and that was to have as many babies as possible. Talk about being brain washed, this seemed to be the ultimate domination that had existed for a thousand years. I don't believe in any religion and could care less about any of them; and I am only expressing a personal opinion.

We worked our way up through Texas visiting places Lorraine remembered as a child and on to Fort Worth where she was born and lived until the family left for Kansas when she was twelve years old. We went to New Mexico, went through the Carlsbad Caverns. We saw the Grand Canyon in Arizona, the Zion National Park in Utah, on to Salt Lake, then home to Boise. It had been a wonderful experience.

We arrived back in Boise in the spring of 1971 and spent two or three weeks in a KOA campground, just resting and visiting friends. Our youngest son Bob was graduating from the University of Idaho at Moscow, Idaho so, of course, we went to the graduation. Thanks to the perseverance of their Mother, all four of the children had college degrees. It hadn't been easy for them or for us financially, even though they worked during the summer months. We still were obligated for over twenty thousand dollars in loans from our credit unions. However, this effort on all our parts made each of them self supporting and probably saved us money in the long run, since we didn't have to help subsidize them when they bought homes, furniture or cars.

After Bob's graduation we got in touch with a couple from the caravan trip to Mexico and the four of us pulled our trailers to Lake Pend Oreille in northern Idaho. This is one of the most beautiful spots in the country and we spent over a month fishing. We smoked the fish, then canned them. These were kokanee, a land locked salmon. They were about eight or nine inches long, and when smoked eight of them would just fit into a quart canning jar. We planned to go to Cleveland, Ohio to visit Kay, but went back to Boise first so that we could welcome Stan's new baby into the world. Finally after saying "Hello" to our new granddaughter, we left. Again with no time schedule we visited many places of interest, Mount Rushmore, where the presidents heads are carved into the rock cliffs, the badlands and on to East Grand Forks, Minnesota. Our crew bombardier had retired and was now living in this city. It was a nice reunion with him and his wife; and they took us to dinner at their local country club. We went back to their home where he set a fifth of good bourbon whiskey on the table and we proceeded to fight the great war over again. About one o'clock our wives deserted us, with Lorraine going out to the trailer and going to bed. We flew some more missions over again and I finally said goodbye and went out to the trailer also. I felt good, not the least bit sleepy and told Lorraine I was going to drive awhile. Their house was at the end of a lane some three hundred feet long and I backed our trailer back out this lane with no problem, which I probably would have had a hard time doing in the daylight and sober. I drove for several miles and finally stopped at a service station for gas. I still felt no pain so drove for another couple of hours.

Finally, getting tired, I pulled off the road and went back to the trailer. I asked Lorraine to get up and find out where we were when daylight came and went to sleep. I woke up three or four hours later and found we were in East Grand Forks, Minnesota. I couldn't believe this, but apparently when I gassed up and in the dark, had turned the wrong way going all the way back. Things like this were almost enough to make me give up drinking. Lorraine has gleefully recounted this understandable mistake that anyone could have made many times, with everyone laughing at my expense. How embarrassing! You would think that if she had any love in her heart, she would forget it. By driving in the daytime we did get to Cleveland, Ohio. Kay and her husband Jon had two children, a girl and a boy. We spent a couple of weeks there getting acquainted with these grandchildren, then headed for St. Petersburg, Florida, where I had taken basic training. The hotel was still there where we had stayed and all this brought back many memories, none of them very good. We found a nice trailer park and because it was winter at home in Idaho we decided to stay until spring. For something to do Lorraine got a job in the hospital laboratory as a microbiologist; and I was going to work on a charter deep sea fishing boat helping the tourists bait their hooks, clean their fish and whatever else needed done. With tips and wages it was a hell of a deal getting paid for going fishing. We had our Thanksgiving dinner in a fancy restaurant with all the trimmings. Somehow it wasn't the same, as it was the first time we had spent this special day alone, not being surrounded by our children, grandchildren and a few friends. The high point of Lorraine's year had been spending three or four days baking pies, cooking turkey, making the best dressing and gravy in the world. For the first time we felt alone. Shortly after Thanksgiving we received a registered letter from the buyer of our housing project stating that he was losing tenants, and he wanted to pay us interest only until he could recover. We were not too surprised since we had met the buyer. He was an accountant and in talking to some of our old tenants who still lived there, they were getting disgusted with all the new rules. We had spoiled them with our eat, drink and be merry attitude in management. Anyway we worried about this and finally decided to go home. It probably wasn't necessary because there was nothing to be done that couldn't be handled by mail or telephone. Secretly we were homesick.

We picked the straightest route from Florida to Idaho and got to Laramie, Wyoming where we ate breakfast and the weather was perfect, with blue skies and fairly warm. West of Laramie the freeway was built over the top of Elk mountain. We were going along the freeway making good time when we passed a sign saying, "Possible extreme high wind ahead". After about fifteen miles Lorraine said, "If the wind's going to blow, it better get started". So it did. We were suddenly in a ground blizzard that even though it wasn't snowing, the wind was picking up the snow on the ground and driving it across the highway. It was just like someone had thrown a white sheet over the windshield and the driving snow coming across from left to right gave me the illusion of running off the road. We didn't dare stop but had to slow down barely moving while Lorraine watched the edge of the pavement to keep me on the road. Suddenly, a young man was in the road, and flagged us down saying his car wouldn't run. We probably saved his life as it had also become very cold. He sat on the passenger side of the car and had to keep the window down so he could see the edge. We crawled along and finally came to an exit and to a service station, where we managed to pull the trailer around out of the wind. My left shoulder was covered with the fine snow that had been driven past the tight window and into the car.

One of the side windows on the trailer had been completely blown out. I had never seen or been in such a blizzard. It finally cleared up enough that the service station owner told us and the several other car and truck owners that we should go on. We all still crept along and finally got to Rawlins, Wyoming. We pulled into a trailer park with everything frozen up and a good inch of ice caked on the front of the trailer. We did have an electrical hook-up so that we could turn the furnace on. We covered the broken window as best as we could and melted the ice off the front of the trailer with a bucket of hot water. We made a hot cup of coffee and some food. Lorraine likes bourbon in her coffee, so we both had a couple of good stiff drinks, which we sure as hell needed. We managed to make about another hundred miles to Rock Springs, the next day, driving on ice covered roads all the way. Lorraine made a comment how good it would be to get through Wyoming and I was compelled to tell her to just be quiet since her last remark had caused the wind to start blowing. The trailer had two wheels on each side and I could see that one of the trailer tires had gone flat and the other one was carrying all the load. I saw no point in worrying her but I knew that if the other one blew out, we wouldn't be going anywhere, at least not with the trailer. But, we did make it into Rock Springs, spent the night, got the trailer tire fixed and headed for Evanston, Wyoming and on into Ogden, Utah, then home to Boise. In all of our travels this had been the worst experience that we had. However, all's well that ends well and we got to Boise without further trouble.

The buyers of our project had completely destroyed our "live and let live" philosophy and as a result had too many vacancies for the project to be able to make a profit. He filed a lawsuit against us over some wording in a

for sale description of the property; and even though it was frivolous, we
had to defend ourselves. It took almost eight months of worry but finally
the court ruled in our favor and directed the buyer to make up all back
payments with interest and also because of his default, he was ordered to
pay all sums owed on the balance.

Even though our R.V. traveling was great, we also knew that we had to
have a home base to come back to and to have enough room for the children to bring their families for a visit. With the settlement we had enough
money to buy four acres on the rim overlooking the valley. We had the
ground excavated for a full basement with a yard in back of the lower level
and the main floor at ground level. The house was designed with large
picture windows on both floors. We moved the trailer to the site and spent
most of the summer doing what we could and hired subcontractors to help.
By early fall we had a nice three bedroom house with a full basement and
one of the best views in the valley. We didn't think we would ever need the
full four acres so kept enough for our home and advertised the balance for
sale. We had moved into the house, so we advertised the Airstream Trailer
for sale too. It sold quickly for almost as much money as we had paid for it.
It was sad to see it go, after almost two years of it being our home and
traveling thousands of miles in it, but fate stepped in again as the Holiday
Rambler travel trailer dealer's son-in-law was a builder and wanted the
ground we had for sale to build houses on. Rim property had gotten scarce
and was getting quite valuable and we ended up trading for a brand new
Holiday, Presidential Model Trailer plus getting ten thousand dollars in
cash. The trailer was a beauty and we got excited again to travel. We spent
many wonderful years going out to Sekiu, Washington each fall salmon
fishing. We drove the Alcan Highway through Canada and on to Alaska.
We went down the Baja peninsula in Mexico and spent a couple of months
each year with eight or ten friends with trailers at Puerto Penasco or "Rocky
Point" as it was called on the mainland of Mexico.

It is an accepted fact that as people get older they have a tendency to live
in the past. I find this is true as I sit and look back over the years. It is with

a great sense of wonderment, when I recall the many dangerous places I had worked. I remember the terror felt during the war seeing planes go down in flames taking the lives of ten young men with them. And the greatest wonderment of all is: Why was I spared and what brought me to this time in life? After almost sixty years of a loving relationship with Lorraine, both of us are still healthy and surrounded by our four children and grandchildren and even twelve great grandchildren, all of whom show us and give us tremendous respect and love.

One of my grand-daughters, Kim wrote the following poem for me in 1995.

MY GRANDFATHER

When I see my grandfather, I see
A quiet man, a tall man, a laughing man,
a striped shirt man,
a white-haired man.

When I smell my grandfather, I smell
A rough pipe, a brown chair, a bag of sweet tobacco,
dark coffee,
and white hair.

When I hear my grandfather, I hear
His laughter and teasing, a childhood name, a gravely voice
A throat-clearing cough,
and rustling white hair.

When I think of my grandfather, I wonder
about the photos with vaguely familiar but un-nameable faces,
about the jokes I didn't always understand,
about the airplane with the lady,
and about how he came to be a miner, a "poacher" and a white-haired man.

When I think of my grandfather, I want people to know
that he works hard, that he writes poems, that he fought in a war,
that he likes to shop from home,
and that he used his hand to straighten his white hair.

When I think of the man I know today as "grandpa", I think
of his travels with grandma, a purple doll, family photos on a shelf,
and I reflect upon a man I never know and never will:
A man who adds goodness to our lives every day he is here
but who lived life that I will never know
before he became the man who is my grandpa with white hair.

Love, Kim

When we celebrated our fifty fifth wedding anniversary I suggested to Lorraine that on our sixtieth, we go back to the little church and re-new our wedding vows with all our family and friends there. Then throw one huge party. When she didn't reply, I looked over and said "What!". "Well", she replied "I'm not sure I want to do that again." I can't believe this. Do you suppose this woman, after sixty years, would be having second thoughts?

In any case, these are truly the golden years. Our days are spent taking a drive or going to the mall. Most mornings, we each get up when the spirit moves us, drink our coffee and read practically every word of the local paper. I remember, when going through the hectic years, that our paper was only glanced at. We glanced at the headlines or maybe an article that claimed our interest, but never had time to sit and absorb all the news locally and from around the world.

Occasionally, now, one or another of our children or grandchildren stops to see us. It seems like they need to touch our peace and tranquillity in order to continue in their own busy lives. Our daughter, Kay and our youngest son Bob live in Boise. Our oldest son, Steve divides his time between summers in Boise and winters in Palm Springs, California. Our middle son, Stan lives in Mesa, Arizona, where we had visited so often, that we decided to buy a home there, where we could spend time with this part of the family and at the same time get out of the cold weather. This way of life seemed like a good arrangement; and now we have the best of both worlds. We leave Idaho the first part of October and come back to our home in Boise about the first of April We have become "snow birds" in every way and migrate south, like the birds in the winter, and north to Idaho for the summer.

We felt so fortunate to be able to spend our time alternating between families, looking forward to seeing one group, then six months later being back with the other. I have come to the conclusion that some of the many benefits of a long term relationship are the memories each of us have and the time to sit and share them together. No marriage is ever without controversy or hardship, but it just seems that more and more of the young people lack the will and or the courage to take a strong stand against adversity. We certainly did take such a stand and are now reaping the rewards of this. So the days pass with complete contentment and lack of any anxieties.

One morning when we planned to go to the mall, Lorraine made the remark that she had a slight headache and would rather stay home. This was not a problem; whether we went to the mall or stayed home was completely immaterial. She had never been prone to headaches, so after they persisted for three or four days, we made an appointment with a neurologist, thinking it was maybe sinuses or some other minor problem. Several tests were done, and finally an M.R.I. showed a tumor in the brain. It was inoperable and not subject to any other treatment because of its deep location. She lasted less than three months, while I sat by her side, holding her hand and desperately trying to pass my strength and even my life to her. The pain became terrible. Not even strong drugs could help; and she pleaded with me to help her die.

One morning I was asleep in the chair by the side of her bed when she squeezed my hand, and in a clear voice said, "I've always loved you" and died.

Someone said to me with compassion,
"Aren't the flowers beautiful?"
And I could only reply,
I guess so, What are they?"
Just to make conversation.

It's been a long trying day,
but at last I sit here alone,
knowing she has really gone away
and will never again come home.
The beautiful flowers with their smell
only add to the despair of my private hell.

Because the inevitable time has come,
with no further escape from reality.
Friends and children bowed with sorrow,
who have stood with nothing to say,
will all be gone tomorrow.

So now, I become nothing again,
performing the motions from habit.
Here memory becomes a curse,
and alcohol may become the nurse,
that prevents my becoming insane.

I lay in my bed at night and sometimes I think that I hear the mournful, compelling sounds of the train whistles, calling, "Come along with me e e e e e; come along with me e e e e e" as I did before I left the Jackson's house. I seem to hear the sound of Lorraine's voice, carried by the wind and I wish I could go.

Did you borrow this book?

Want a copy of your own?

Need a great gift for a friend or loved one?

Yes, I want to have a personal copy of this book. Please send me
_____ copies of *The Orphan.*

Please add $2.50 per book for postage and handling. Idaho residents include 5% state sales tax in the amount of $.90 per book. Send check payable to :

Chet Hosac
5820 N. Cloud Nine Drive
Boise, Idaho 83714
(208) 378–7088

Print Name _____

Address _____

City _____ State _____ Zip _____

The Orphan $17.95 x ___ # books = _____

Postage and Handling $2.50 x ___ # books = _____

Idaho Tax $ .90 x ___ # books = _____

Enclosed is my check/money order
for the total amount of $ _____

Quantity Orders Invited

Please photo copy this page if additional forms are needed.